Psyche

By: Athena Chao

EliteLink Publishing | New York City

Psyche

Cover Design By: Isis Wai-Hernandez

Paperback ISBN: 979-8-9932184-9-6

eBook ISBN: 979-8-9932184-8-9

Author's Note

I wish I could say Psyche began with a single, brilliant idea that arrived fully formed. Instead, it has been an excruciating labor of love resulting from something that began more as a messy pile of chaotic thoughts that refused to leave me alone. It started with a few disconnected scenes followed by a character I couldn't stop thinking about. Add to that a lot of "wait, what if..." moments, and the meandering journey stubbornly turned into a story. Somewhere along the way, I realized I had gone from casually daydreaming to writing an entire novel.

And what a "novel" experience, am I right?

Writing this book meant getting very comfortable with not knowing what I was doing. I am not a pro outliner. The plot changed, the characters changed, and sometimes it felt like they understood themselves better than I understood them. I ruthlessly scrapped them out of thin air and sheer frustration at not being able to write any personality into them. I spent countless hours chasing ideas, rewriting scenes, and wondering if everything would ever come together in the end.

At its core, Psyche is about the unknown. It represents the parts of the world we cannot fully explain, and the parts of ourselves we are still figuring out. I've always been drawn to that space (pardon the pun) because it's where the most interesting possibilities live.

But I need to give a little credit to the team that got me here. I owe some heartfelt thanks to:

- My dad, for editing my story and uncovering all the plot holes I somehow managed to dig without noticing;

- My mom, for patiently listening to me rant about the plot, and its ever-expanding holes, despite having no idea what I was talking about;
- Zenith, for finally escaping the depths of perfect-protagonist prison; and
- The music artists I wrote to, like G.E.M. and I-DLE;

And, for reasons that are and will remain a mystery to my lovely readers.

If you've ever felt unsure of what's ahead, or secretly think the unknown might be more fun than the known, I hope this story gives you a place to get a little lost in...on purpose.

- Athena Chao

Table of Contents

Chapter 1

There was a girl on the ship. She had been there for as long as anyone could remember, yet nobody could seem to recall who she was. She was a scrawny little thing, with long, wavy brown hair that dragged along after her in a tangled mess, and empty, faded green eyes that seemed to be watching something. Or someone.

She never spoke. She didn't eat much either, only appearing at odd hours in the corridors, sometimes leaning against a wall as if waiting for something invisible, sometimes staring at the air above the control panels, her gaze unblinking. Her presence was so persistent, so silent, that it became a part of the ship's background, like the faint hum of the engines or the low vibration of the gravity stabilizers.

Nobody paid her any attention. Most crew members simply passed her by, pretending not to notice. Some whispered rumors. Maybe she was a ghost. Maybe she had been born aboard the ship, some accident of the universe. Some said she was the ship itself, manifest in human form. Some said she knew more than anyone would dare suspect, always present yet unnoticed, almost as if she were a pulse in the ship's own mind.

There was another girl on that ship. She was not quite as young as the first, but still innocent and naive; much unlike the first. She worked aboard the spaceship as an assistant, hired by the Chief Engineer because his old assistant had been eaten by an alien bird. This girl's name was Min.

Or at least that was what everyone called her.

"Min!"

An exasperated voice echoed through the metal halls.

"Coming!" she called back, hurriedly descending the winding stairs and clambering down the slippery metal ladders. Her boots clanged against the steel rungs as she went, the sound echoing ominously in the cavernous engine level.

From the corner of her vision, she caught the faint glimmer of someone else—a shadow, unmoving, standing at the landing above, watching. For a moment, she froze, the hairs on the back of her neck rising. She blinked, and the figure seemed to disappear.

She entered a room that smelled and felt like metal. The smell clung to her clothes instantly, a mixture of hot metal and fuel mingling with something sharper, like the tang of scorched circuits. Three tiny desks were covered in a spread of screwdrivers, drills, shattered tablet screens, and maybe a wrench or two buried in the mess. The floor was littered with stray wires and scorch marks from experiments gone awry. The room ended in a flimsy iron railing, the only thing separating the engineers from the glowing circular generator that powered the entire ship.

The spaceship was named Horizon-2, after the vanguard ship sent to explore the edge of the known universe, only to disappear without a trace. The Alliance of Sentient Sapiens, otherwise known as the ASS, was hoping to discover more about the universe after the futile efforts of Horizon-1. Min often wondered if the naming committee had been drunk or just had a horrendously bad sense of humor.

"Min!" A voice shouted, pulling her out of her thoughts. "Stop zoning out and hand me a wrench!"

The voice belonged to the Chief Engineer, Zenith, tall and lean with an aura of unspoken authority that seemed almost inhuman. His long, wavy white hair shimmered faintly in the glow of the machinery, and a glittering teal gemstone was embedded in his forehead. His eyes were bright, sharp, and unreadable, like the depths of a storm-tossed sea. Standing at six feet tall, he was short by his race's standards, but his presence filled the room regardless.

Min sorted through the mess of tools on the desks, finally retrieving the wrench he had asked for. She tossed it at him, muttering under her breath about the state of the workshop.

Chapter 1

He caught it swiftly, just before the handle of the wrench could smack him in the head. He glared at her. "Do you realize how dangerous that was? You could've—"

"Knocked your precious consciousness out of your body. Yeah, yeah. I know the story. Your ancestors found a way to condense their souls into gemstones that they welded to artificially created bodies in order to achieve almost-immortality. But if you were to lose your gem, your body would reanimate itself using the remaining power of your consciousness; the corruption turning you into a Nirvaelith. Or in the worst-case scenario, I would damage it, it would go kaboom, and we'd all get blown to bits." She looked at him pointedly. "Did I miss anything?"

"You missed the part where you could've just knocked me out." He replied, turning back to his work, a wisp of a smile tugging at the edge of his lips.

"I dream of the day that actually happens." She plopped onto a nearby stool and leaned over his shoulder, trying to catch a glimpse of the tangle of wires he was working on. "Anyways, what are you doing?"

"Someone rewired the heating system of the left wing. Now half the crew can't go to bed without twelve pounds of blankets wrapped around them." He glared at her.

"Would you believe me if I said it wasn't me?"

The Chief Engineer set down the wrench and turned to face her.

"Now, Min. You said you wanted to learn something on this ship." He leaned in, long, slender fingers tilting her chin up. "I think the first thing you need to learn is common sense. And observation, patience, and perhaps, how to notice the things that no one else looks for."

He flicked her on the forehead.

"Ow!"

"You and I are the only two people with access to this place." He gestured dramatically at the expansive metal room. "If I didn't do it, I wonder who did."

"You told me to connect the blue ones! That's what I did!" Min protested, pointing at some of the wires.

The Chief Engineer made a face. "Those are teal. These—" he pointed to the two slightly darker blue wires that were almost completely hidden by the tangled mess of other wires. "—are blue."

Before Min could protest, her comms watch buzzed. She tapped it vehemently, and a small holographic screen flickered to life above her wrist.

"Cap wants to speak to your boss," the voice said. It was informal, casual, but tense. Something in the tone made Min feel a chill.

"Then call him, don't call me, Lance!" she shouted.

"Dude, his comms watch is on silent," the voice deadpanned. "No, no, no—Cap—dude, get your own watch—this is mine—"

A booming voice suddenly filled the room, echoing off the metal walls.

"Answer your damn calls, Zenith! I didn't invite you on this ship to ignore my messages! I only asked for you because they said you were the best engineer in the alliance!" It was the Captain, and his annoyance was real.

"Uh-huh. I've heard that excuse many times already. Care to explain why I'm still here even though I annoy the hell out of you?" Zenith continued to fiddle with the wires. "You just love me so much you can't get rid of me."

The voice on the other end grumbled something profane.

Zenith was unbothered. "Don't delude yourself, my dear captain. I'm a few hundred years older than you'll probably ever get. I know denial when I see it."

"And yet, here you are, working for me." The Captain tsk'd, feigning disappointment. "But this is serious, and I need you at the bridge ASAP."

His message delivered, the Captain hung up. Zenith let out a long, exasperated sigh, wiping sweat and grime from his brow. He grabbed Min's wrist, tugging her toward the exit.

"To the bridge we go, then."

"I can walk myself, you know?" She struggled to get out of his grip.

He put a finger to her lips. "Shush, sweetheart. Captain says this is serious."

As they moved through the corridors, the hum of the ship seemed alive, almost aware of them, wrapping around their footsteps like a second heartbeat. Min thought she glimpsed that mysterious figure again, standing at the edge of the maintenance hatch, her eyes glimmering unnaturally. She blinked, and the figure was gone. But the sense of being watched lingered.

Min focused on Zenith's lecture on the difference between teal and blue wires, trying hard not to trip over the uneven metal flooring.

"This ship is a mess," Min muttered, as her foot caught on another uneven metal plate, almost tripping.

"Not a mess," he corrected sharply. "It's in a state of beautiful chaos."

Min gave him a skeptical look. "I think you're just saying that because you don't want to admit it's falling apart."

Zenith rolled his eyes. "If it were falling apart, you'd already be gone in a puff—" he made a hand motion like an explosion. "—of cosmic radiation. The ship will endure. It always does. Horizon-2 won't let go of her crew like her predecessor."

Min had zoned out. Once again, her foot caught on the uneven metal plating, but this time, she was not prepared to stop herself before she fell over. Her face was nearly an inch from the floor when Zenith caught her forearm, successfully preventing her from faceplanting.

"Did you just fall for me, sweetheart?"

Min grumbled one of those human curse words that just rolled right off the tongue so easily.

"Language," Zenith chided, pulling her back up.

"Since when did you know the meaning of fu—"

He slapped a hand over her mouth. "I know that it's a commonly used expletive on Earth, and I also know that it means to 'screw' with someone."

She nodded, hoping that he would release her, all the time unsure where he had learned that and who had taught it to him, but she frankly didn't care. Finally, Zenith took his hand off her mouth, wiping it along Min's shoulder seam. They kept walking. The ship hummed along, keeping pace with the beat of her heart in a rhythm that was almost reassuring. Almost.

Finally, they reached the elevator. Zenith pressed a panel, and the doors slid open smoothly. It appeared as if the engine room was the only area of the ship that was in dire need of maintenance.

The figure lingered, encased in shadow, emerald eyes watching from an alcove in the corridor. Min felt their gaze even before she turned to look.

Inside the elevator, Zenith flicked open the service switch and stabbed his key into the slot.

"Want to do this the boring way or the fun way?"

Before Min could provide him with an answer he wasn't going to bother hearing anyway, Zenith turned the key clockwise and quickly removed it from its slot, shoving it in his pocket just before the gravity turned off. They rose upwards, Min holding onto Zenith's arm for dear life, as the air, free from the constraints of artificial gravity, sent the two of them slowly bouncing around in the vacuum of the elevator shaft, giving neither of them any sort of foothold.

"I'm surprised you haven't tried this yet, sweetheart."

"I haven't tried it because I VALUE MY LIFE—" Her sentence ended in a piercing scream as the gravity returned suddenly.

Zenith flinched.

"We're here. You can stop squeezing my arm."

Min let go. "Oh. Whoops."

The doors opened. The bridge sprawled out in front of them: lights, screens, and operators, each absorbed in their respective tasks. The Captain stood at the center, arms crossed. The air hummed with more than the engines. Min's stomach twisted. The little girl's shadow lingered near the corner, unseen by others, yet impossible to ignore for Min. Something was waiting. Something she knew wasn't going to be good.

CHAPTER 2

By the time Zenith and Min arrived at the bridge, almost the entire crew had already gathered there, with the exception of the doctor, nurse, and one of the members of the research team. The bridge itself buzzed with a low, vibrating energy, as though the ship were holding its breath in anticipation. Every light flickered slightly, casting elongated shadows that slithered along the walls like living things.

The Captain, Cronanu Zor—better known to the crew as Cronan, or simply "Cap," and to some of his closer friends as "old man"—was perched on his chair, tapping his foot impatiently. Each tap echoed unnaturally across the metal floor, the sound amplified by the reinforced alloy of the bridge, making it seem louder than it should have been. Cronan was Triskelion, an alien race known for their wisdom and insect-like appearance, with their three eyes and four arms. The glimmering carapace of his exoskeleton reflected the lights of the control panels, giving him a faint aura that made him seem almost iridescent, like a jewel, or a rainbow. Though Triskelions lived almost ten times as long as humans, Cronan was rather young for his species at only 150 years old. At present, he looked like a scarab beetle in a captain's hat and an ill-fitting uniform.

The Weapons Master, Lancer Kedge, a half-cyborg obsessed with vintage tasers, was also present. He had lost the left side of his body in a generator accident early in his career. Currently, he was slouched in the corner, fiddling with his new weapons control panel, muttering to himself. The mechanical hum of his cybernetic arm blended with the ship's ambient noise, creating a rhythm that matched the low thrum of the engines.

Next to him sat Quori, the Head Scientist, desperately trying to prevent Lance from "accidentally" activating something catastrophic. Her six fingers twitched whenever he was about to press something. She was a Thalassarii, an alien race known for their photographic memory and extremely heightened senses, with some that humans did not possess. The Weapons Master was a little too trigger-happy for the poor scientist's liking. Her glasses reflected data streams from multiple screens at once, her eyebrows furrowed together in deep thought.

At the far end of the room stood Liran Phost, the Chief Communications Specialist, along with her assistant, Jace Voss. Liran was a Noophon from the Lexicon System, a hyper-linguistic species specializing in learning languages and decoding ciphers, who also happened to closely resemble horned Star Wars characters. Each planet of the system housed a different Noophon variant, and Liran hailed from Lexicon-8, home of the blue Noophons, known for rapid translation of foreign and alien tongues. Jace, however, was still trying to figure out which end of a translation tablet was up.

The two pilots of Horizon-2, Xy'vaal and Juno, octopus and cyborg, whispered nervously near the large viewport at the front. Every so often, one of them would point at something on the shared monitor and glance at the captain for confirmation. Xy'vaal's eight-limbed form shifted with uncanny fluidity, a blur of movement and thought, while Juno's simple-minded intensity contrasted starkly. Yet both exuded the tension of individuals who could sense danger long before its arrival. At one point, Xy'vaal patted Juno on the back with a limb while simultaneously solving a Rubik's cube under the table, the movements almost impossible for anyone else to track. Must be the perk of having two brains.

Zenith dragged Min into the room, and almost immediately, a small purple blob leapt at her face, smearing her with a slimy citrus-scented goo.

"Gloop!" she exclaimed when she finally disentangled herself from the little octopus-like creature's tentacles. Gloop's tiny body glowed a cheerful yellow, radiating warmth and a simply intangible optimism, despite its slippery mess. The little creature gave a little "woop-woop" and settled into their perch on Min's head.

Gloop was the ship's Janitor. They moved with uncanny efficiency, sliding along walls, ceilings, and floors like a multi-legged snail, cleaning surfaces in patterns that suggested an intelligence beyond simple instinct. The slime trail they left behind evaporated in a faint citrus mist, creating an atmosphere that was oddly comforting in the metallic bridge. These were the perks of being a Plooble, other than simply being cute, of course.

Min had learned soon after joining the crew that Xy'vaal and Gloop were distant relatives, their connection stretching back generations through unknown genetic threads that seemed almost magical in nature, and completely incomprehensible in logic. Because how could a walking, talking octopus be related to a somewhat cephalopod-shaped slime blob?

Cronan called the room to attention, bug arms waving around. "I must congratulate you all on a successful exploratory mission—" hands clapped and echoed against the metal walls, the cascade of sound bouncing in every direction. "—but we are now facing a serious problem. No matter how far we travel towards the Alliance base, the distance displayed on the monitors will not decrease. We are eternally ten light-years from home."

Gasps filled the bridge. Even the youngest crew members, usually impervious to panic, stiffened as if the air itself had become heavier.

"I've got a bad feeling about this," Lance said, his voice casual but firm. "And when my intuition tells me things are gonna go wrong, it's time to pull the trigger."

He raised the weapons panel triumphantly, but Quori was quick to confiscate it from him.

"Have you tried flying in a different direction?" Zenith asked, voice light despite the tension. "For all we know, we might just be circling the base at a constant distance."

"Do you think we haven't tried that already, Mr. Know-it-all?" Juno shot an angry glare at him. "For all we know, the damn screen is faulty!"

Xy'vaal slapped a tentacle over Juno's mouth before she could start spouting curse words of a more profane variety. He smiled innocently. Beneath the table, one limb still twisted the Rubik's cube, tentacles flying in a precise, choreographed movement that no human could match.

Liran piped up. "Have you tried checking the units?"

"The thing is measured in LY. Light Years," Juno grumbled, wrestling herself out of Xy'vaal's iron grip. "What more do you want?"

Jace said, "A sandwich," while Liran said, "Well, you never know."

"Nerds."

A movement in the darkest corner of the bridge caught Min's attention. It was the little girl—the one no one seemed to know anything about. She crouched in a pile of shadow, her hair an untamed tangle, her green eyes gleaming with a strange, silent intelligence. The air around her seemed to turn colder, denser, almost as if she drew the shadows toward her. Min shivered, realizing that no one else seemed to notice.

The Rubik's cube, now solved, sat abandoned, almost like a marker of something completed and waiting. The conversation continued around her, but Min's eyes stayed fixed on the little girl.

"Is it possible that we were hooked on by a tractor beam that we didn't detect?" Lance proposed, still trying to wrestle his prized weapons panel out of Quori's grasp.

Xy'vaal perked up. He checked the ship's outer scan. Slumped. "Nope."

"Aw man." The weapons master sighed, the chance to blast something slipping out from under him.

Quori patted him on the back. "Don't worry, Lance. I'm sure you'll get to 'kick some alien ass,' as you enjoy putting it, someday."

Gloop warbled supportively from their perch on Min's head.

Lance sighed, finally giving up on his failed battle for the weapons panel. "This meeting isn't going anywhere."

"Well, as far as can presently be ascertained, there seems to be no solution to our predicament," Cronan said. "We best continue our work until a solution is found. You may all return to your posts."

The crew dispersed. Lance wandered back to his quarters to tinker, Quori returned to the lab to relay information to the research team, Liran and Jace resumed their puzzle game, and Xy'vaal released Juno from his gentle restraint. The Captain paced around his chair. Gloop returned to cleaning, leaving a faint orange scent in their wake.

Min approached the little girl. "What's your name?" she asked softly.

"Psyche," the girl whispered. Her voice was faint, barely audible, yet it carried an unexpected weight, like a small pebble causing ripples across still water.

"And what are you doing on this ship?"

Before Psyche could respond, a firm hand wrapped around Min's arm, dragging her away.

"Zenith! I have two perfectly working legs! You don't need to drag me everywhere!" Min protested, though she didn't struggle this time. She had learned the futility of arguing, especially when Zenith's grin hinted at a mischief she was helpless against.

"Oh, I know," he said, a ghost of a smile flickering across his face. "I simply enjoy messing with you, sweetheart."

He flicked her lightly on the forehead. Min sighed, half-exasperated, half-enthralled, as the bridge stretched before her, alive with a liveliness she had never felt in the quiet corridors below. And somewhere, in the shadows, Psyche watched. Waiting.

CHAPTER 3

Back in the engine room, Zenith finally released Min from his cold, iron grip. The tension in his hands lingered a moment longer than necessary, a reminder of the quiet authority he carried even in casual moments. He shuffled back to the electric panel, tools clanking softly against the metal floor, returning to his work fixing the tangled mess of wires that seemed to have a life of its own.

Min sat down on the edge of a stool, her legs dangling over the side. She picked up a tablet and scrolled through the alliance database, the pale blue light from its screen painting her face in shades of digital frost. Headlines flickered past, some mundane, some strange—stories of alien encounters, new planets discovered, and human colonies adapting in ways that were barely believable. She paused at a particularly obscure article about a missing ship that had vanished near the edge of a binary star system, Horizon-1. She frowned, her mind nudged by a sense of déjà vu.

Every so often, Zenith called for her assistance. "Min, pass me the red phaser module." She would rise and sift through the disorder of wires, sparks, and metallic scraps for five minutes before triumphantly returning the requested item. Sometimes she felt like a spectator to his chaos, watching a conductor orchestrate a symphony of disarray. Sheer pandemonium wasn't really for her, but watching Zenith, she could see why he called it "beautiful chaos." He was truly beautiful, even if the chaos he caused wasn't.

Finally, after what seemed like hours, he straightened and stepped back from the panel. Zenith stood tall, dusting his sleeves off. He closed the electric panel with a sharp click and examined his right index finger, which had been nicked on the sharp metal edge. A bead of blood formed and clung stubbornly to his skin, catching the dim overhead lights. He poked it experimentally, flinching as it welled further, before bringing it to his mouth to taste the faint metallic tang.

Min noticed him and blinked. Her stomach twisted at the

humanity of the act. When Zenith realized her attention was on him, he abruptly withdrew his finger and crossed his arms, an almost imperceptible flush spreading across his pale cheeks.

"What do you want?" he asked, strolling toward her and plopping into the chair beside her.

"Hm?" Min raised an eyebrow.

"If you don't have anything to say, then what were you watching me for?"

"Oh, yeah. I did want to ask you something," she said cautiously. Her fingers toyed with the edge of the tablet as if it could anchor her courage. "You know that little girl we have on the ship?"

Zenith rested his head gently on her shoulder, his long, glittering lashes fluttering as he closed his eyes. The faint scent of metal and machinery clung to him, mixing oddly with the citrusy remnants of Gloop's cleaning slime.

"Are you talking about yourself?" he murmured.

"What? No!" Min exclaimed, pushing him gently. "Get off me!"

"Letting me rest on your shoulder for a bit isn't going to kill you, sweetheart. Now, what were you saying?"

She let out an exasperated sigh. Sometimes this thousand-year-old alien could behave like a petulant child, testing boundaries in ways that were both infuriating and oddly endearing. He was like a clingy cat, annoying, yet too adorable to ignore. "You know the girl with messy brown hair and green eyes?"

"Yeah. What about her?"

"Do you remember when she boarded the ship?"

"Nope." Zenith replied casually, wrapping his arms around her waist. When Min tried to pry his hands apart, he tightened his hold instantly.

"I'm being serious! Why won't you listen?"

"There's no point in me being serious if you're not talking about a serious topic, sweetheart." He lifted his head, lips brushing her cheek ever so slightly. The gesture was intimate enough to make Min's stomach flutter uncomfortably.

A pause followed, broken by Min's decision: "I'll just ask the others about it."

Zenith straightened, releasing her. "They don't know anything either."

"And how would you know that?"

"Do you honestly think that you're the first person to ever have suspicions about Psyche? Sweetheart, you flatter yourself." He gave her a small, mischievous boop on the nose, punctuating the moment with a gesture meant to disarm. He stood up.

"I think I'm gonna go take a nap. Maybe you should too," he added, stretching before leaving the room. Min watched him go, the empty echo of his boots leaving a silence that seemed heavier than the presence he'd just vacated. Then it hit her—she had never told him Psyche's name.

* * *

Min followed his advice and returned to her room in the right wing. The corridors of the right wing were quieter, narrower, with fewer maintenance noises and more personal spaces for junior officers. The walls were lined with soft metal panels that muffled the faint hum of the ship's core, giving the corridor an almost intimate, protective feel.

She was about to settle down with her book when a sudden, piercing headache forced her to collapse onto the floor. The pain clawed through her skull, and a black curtain closed over her vision, dragging her consciousness into the darkness hiding in her mind.

Chapter 3

When she opened her eyes, she could barely make out the dim outlines of two figures and what appeared to be a laboratory. Everything shimmered with a strange distortion, as if the air itself had become thick and viscous with slime. Shadows moved along the walls independently, curling and stretching in ways that made the room seem alive and real.

"She is far from perfect. You cannot subject her to such tests." The man on the left spoke softly, voice gentle like the father Min never had. His form was partially obscured by a long, flowing trench coat, which her mind insisted was vintage, though she could not recall from where it had drawn that conclusion.

"That is of little significance. If we succeed, she will be unstoppable. We will have created the strongest and smartest creature to ever exist!" The second man's voice was grating, sharp enough to scrape against her nerves. Even the shadows seemed to recoil from it.

"But she will not be perfect. Her body is but a shell too simple to contain the emotions her mind craves. She cannot feel love, yet she yearns for it, as all humans do. That yearning will become her undoing."

The man on the right crossed his arms. His lab coat gleamed unnaturally in the dim, green light, the pristine fabric a stark contrast to the darkness surrounding them. "Love is built on trust. If she cannot trust anyone, how will she ever know love? How will she ever desire it if she will never know it?"

"But—"

"You knew what you were signing up for when you agreed to this contract. Project Minerva must not fail. You will do as I say, or I will expose your identity to the rest of the known world." The lab-coated man strode out, leaving the room.

The first man collapsed to the floor, head in hands, voice quivering with regret. "I'm sorry. I'm so, so sorry." Min's chest tightened at the sound, memories of similar scenes flooding her mind like a tide she had fought to suppress.

But then he said something she had never heard before. Something subtle, almost whispered, that cut through the fog of the world. "What will he think of me when he hears about this?"

The edges of Min's vision began to fade. The laboratory blurred, its contours melting into darkness. Only the soft, echoing sobs of the man remained, distant and haunting.

Then everything fell silent, leaving her to the mercy of her own thoughts, dreams, and fears. A faint whisper, delicate and thread-like, wove itself into her consciousness:

"Oh, you poor little thing. Strung between two worlds like a puppet on a string."

Even this voice chose to abandon her, leaving Min suspended in a void between reality and dream. Her mind floated, untethered, in the half-light of perception and imagination, waiting for something, someone, to anchor her back to the present.

CHAPTER 4

"Min!"

A voice was calling her. It echoed through the fog in her mind like a distant bell, fraying the silence around her. It was nice to know that someone still cared. The voice grew desperate.

"Please wake up, please..."

Someone was shaking her. Min opened her eyes. The world swam into focus slowly, as though she were dragging herself up through deep water. Her head felt heavier than lead and she groaned as she sat up.

"Ow..." She rubbed her temples, unaware of the person kneeling beside her.

Zenith cleared his throat, making Min jump with surprise. His eyes had a liquid sheen to them as if he had almost cried. For a moment, he looked unusually fragile, as though something in her collapse had cracked open a part of him he didn't show anyone. He touched the back of his hand to her forehead.

"You don't have a temperature. What happened?"

"Nothing...nothing!" She backed away from him and stood up quickly. "I'm perfectly fine. There's no need for you to worry."

Zenith gave her a disbelieving look.

"I'm fine. I promise!"

He stood up and stepped toward her slowly. "Are you sure? Do you need visit the Medbay?"

"No!"

Zenith raised a single eyebrow.

"I'm fine. Really."

Before Min could react, he wrapped his arms around her legs and hoisted her over his shoulder. The motion was effortless, a sudden reminder that his deceptively slim frame hid the strength of an alien species far older than she could imagine.

"Let me down! Where are you taking me?" She pounded on his back, but he didn't budge.

"Stop resisting, sweetheart. I'm taking you to Medbay."

Min considered biting him. Actually sinking her teeth into his shoulder. She wasn't sure if Vaelithari skin tasted metallic, floral, or vaguely toxic, but at this point she was willing to find out. Unfortunately, Zenith's grip tightened subtly, as if he could sense her violent little thought and was preemptively securing her like a misbehaving cat.

"Don't even try it," he warned without looking at her.

"I wasn't going to!"

"Your heart rate spiked," he said dryly. "Whenever you get ideas, your heart rate jumps to 140. Very useful diagnostics."

Min gasped. "You can hear that?"

"It doesn't help that you're literally pressed against me," Zenith replied. "It's quite loud and it's giving you away."

Min groaned into his back. Of course he would notice these insignificant details. Who knew how long it would be before he figured out how she felt about him?

* * *

Kairos Blythe, a Triskelion and the ship's doctor, had a personality much like that of a mad scientist. Unique and peculiar things interested her, and she could get a little unhinged when excited. Nonetheless, she was very good at her job. Her Medbay was cluttered with antique books, strange biological samples suspended in glowing jars, and handwritten notes taped to the walls in chaotic constellations.

She had been flipping through an old 21st-century science magazine when Zenith arrived, carrying a very unwilling Min. Kairos' eyes lit up.

"So what brings you two here?" she asked, tucking away her magazine. She flicked Zenith on the forehead. "Last I remember, you said that you had better things to do than visit an old lady like me."

Zenith ignored the jab and gently deposited Min onto the examination table—though Min would have argued that there was nothing gentle about it.

"She fainted earlier. Can you check to see if she's alright? She insists that she's fine, but I disagree."

The doctor smiled and called for her assistant.

"Wren!"

Wren Solace was the second-youngest crew member, second only to Min. He was a 30-year-old human, which was as boring as it got. According to Min's observations, she suspected he had a crush on Kairos, a thought that disturbed her greatly because of the huge age gap between them, and not to be racist, but she just couldn't stomach the thought of a human and a beetle making out. Wren arrived breathless, hair slightly disheveled in the way of someone trying desperately to make a good impression.

"Why don't you keep this lovely old man busy for a bit?" Kairos said, shooing them away. Zenith rolled his eyes, reluctantly following the young nurse into the adjacent room. Kairos was well aware of Wren's feelings, though she wasn't sure how she felt about him yet. For the moment, she enjoyed teasing him.

Kairos checked Min's temperature half-heartedly, and when that revealed nothing, she initiated a full-body scan. Min had been very opposed to the scan, and Kairos only succeeded after several minutes of coaxing. Throughout the entire process, Min sat stiffly, fidgeting with her hands.

"I think you're fine. Nothing seems wrong here." Kairos studied the information on her tablet. Then something small caught her eye. Her brows furrowed, the joking glimmer in her expression snapping away as her posture stiffened. She immediately pulled up Min's information page from the ASS database and compared the listed data with the scan results.

"Hmm...that's strange..."

Min straightened, wringing her hands more aggressively than before.

"You're not—"

Just then, Zenith walked back into the room with Wren.

"So?" He said, crossing his arms and leaning casually against the side of the examination table.

Kairos let out an awkward laugh. Her eyes darted toward Min once before sliding away. The young engineer bit her lip. "Everything seems fine. Probably just a really bad headache."

"I see." Zenith did not appear convinced.

"I told you I was fine! There's nothing to worry about," Min insisted.

Zenith opened his mouth to argue—she could tell, because his left ear twitched, a subtle Zenith-style tell of impatience—but he closed it again slowly, eyes narrowing at her in a way that made her feel uncomfortably transparent, like he was trying to read her thoughts straight off her forehead.

"You're lying," he said quietly, only for her to hear.

Min flinched. "I'm not—"

"Sweetheart," he murmured, "you only fidget with your thumbs when you're scared. And you only bite your lip when you're hiding something."

She hadn't realized she was doing either. She stopped abruptly, cheeks heating.

After the two left, Kairos slumped onto the examination table. She picked up the tablet once more to make sure she hadn't misread. But the screen still displayed the same thing.

"What's wrong?" Wren asked, leaning over her shoulder.

"The ASS site says that she's human, but—" Kairos paused. Her eyes darkened, and a rare seriousness overtook her features. She decided that it was best to not tell him what she had noticed. "It's nothing. Probably just a typo."

Wren nodded, though Kairos wasn't sure he believed her. The doctor sighed, dropping the tablet beside her.

"Oh, what a terrible, doomed love story this is."

Wren blinked back at the giant beetle. "Love story?"

Kairos stared dramatically at the ceiling. "A delicate fool of a girl with too many secrets, and a man who's too clever to let her keep any of them."

"You mean Zenith?"

She snorted. "Of course I mean Zenith. You think I'm talking about you? Don't be ridiculous. You're a child."

Wren sputtered. "I'm thirty—"

"Exactly." Kairos waved him off.

* * *

It is a well-known fact that the Vaelithari can extend their lifespans indefinitely by switching between bodies. They have specialized scientists called corpse-crafters who possess the unique ability to create bodies to house the gemstones containing their consciousness. But if a discarded body is not disposed of, usually by incineration, the remnants of the Vaelithari soul may reanimate the corpse, resulting in Nirvaeliths.

These corrupted Vaelithari bodies appear identical to their uncorrupted counterparts, save for the absence of the gemstone on their foreheads. Centuries ago, the Vaelithari fought a long war against the Nirvaeliths on Vaelea, discovering that the bodies would never disappear unless completely destroyed or the original gemstone was shattered.

After the war, Vaelithari scientists spent decades creating a mechanism to detect Nirvaeliths, who had learned how to disguise the absence of their gemstones. From then on, all ASS medical equipment was equipped with this technology to root out hidden Nirvaeliths among the general population.

The Vaelithari claim the Nirvaeliths are corruption incarnate. But if a body has a soul—Vaelithari or otherwise—is that being not alive? Is that being still a Nirvaelith?

—from Dr. Lysander Cale's notes about Project Minerva

CHAPTER 5

It was dinner time, and the spaceship's lounge, a moderately small room on the top floor of Horizon-2, was sparsely littered with members of the crew, each person browsing through the limited selection of food options. The faint hum of the ship's life support system filled the room, mingling with the clatter of trays and the occasional murmur of casual conversation. A soft golden light reflected off the polished metallic surfaces, casting shadows that danced across the room in rhythm with the spaceship's gentle sway.

Min entered, followed closely by Zenith, still carrying a subtle tension of unease about his assistant's health. Each step she took echoed softly against the floor, drawing the attention of a few crew members before they returned to their conversations or food. As soon as they walked in, Cronan disentangled himself from the one-sided conversation Liran, the comms specialist, had been having with him about the relationships between alien languages. The Captain's face lit up, and he moved toward the two engineers with his usual easy charm, clearly pleased to have an excuse to speak with someone else.

"How are things going, Zenith? Did you fix the heating issue?" Cronan asked, his voice carrying that warm, teasing undertone he always used with his crew. He placed an arm around the Chief Engineer's shoulders in an almost brotherly gesture.

Zenith tilted his head slightly, a faint scowl creasing his forehead. "What do you think?"

The Captain chuckled, a deep, rolling sound that seemed to resonate through the small lounge. "I would assume so, but you never know. Maybe one day you'll choose to embrace your spontaneous side. I only hope to be alive to see it."

"Excuse me," Min interrupted, her voice soft but steady, cutting through the playful banter. Both men's heads turned toward her. "I'm gonna go get something to eat if I'm not needed at the moment."

She moved toward the buffet with a measured grace, the fabric of her uniform shifting silently around her. Zenith watched her retreating figure, his mouth open, throat tight. Cronan hummed in mock contemplation.

"I believe there's a human saying for this..." he said, leaning casually against the counter. "I think the phrase is 'cat got your tongue.'"

"My dear captain," Zenith responded, his tone low and sharp, cutting through Cronan's amusement. He flashed his giant bug of a captain a patronizing look. "I'm allergic to cats."

* * *

Min had barely spared the ship's buffet a glance before plopping down on one of the more isolated chairs in the far corner of the room. The seat creaked softly beneath her as she leaned forward, resting her elbows on her knees and her chin in her hands. She let her fingers curl around her face, forming a makeshift cradle for her thoughts, trying to make sense of the strange scene she had seen when her headache had hit her.

Who was the man in the trench coat referring to? The question looped in her mind, spiraling into tangles of half-formed images and fleeting emotions she couldn't quite place.

She thought back to the words that had haunted her: "If she cannot trust anyone, how will she ever know love?" The phrase lingered like the aftertaste of bitter medicine, sharp and impossible to ignore.

Her gaze drifted toward Zenith, who was standing awkwardly, sandwiched between the ever-smiling Cronan and Kairos, the doctor, who had just entered the lounge. He was, quite literally, a beetle sandwich. The slight tension in his shoulders, the barely perceptible tapping of his foot, and the way his jaw tightened as if holding back a sigh spoke to her in ways words could not. That feeling, the one humans call "butterflies in your stomach," stirred within her chest.

Chapter 5

Was it real, this flutter of warmth and tension that Zenith provoked in her? Or was it a trick her mind had invented to fill a longing she barely dared to acknowledge? A longing to be loved, to be cared for, to be understood.

And yet...Zenith understood her. He always had. From the very beginning.

* * *

Min's mind wandered back to the day she had first applied for the assistant engineer position on Horizon-2, years ago. There had been nearly fifty applicants, each diverse in gender, race, and background. She remembered the moment she had first laid eyes on Zenith. His features were delicate yet sharp, his presence commanding even as he remained seated behind a pile of applications that towered on his desk.

That day, her stereotype that all engineers were boring, messy shut-ins had been shattered in an instant.

And perhaps, in the midst of the nervous wreck of her mind, a small blossom of romance had bloomed.

Zenith had barely spared the massive stack of applications a glance. With a flick of his wrist, he had sent them cascading into the shredder beneath his desk, the papers whirring into oblivion. Many applicants had recoiled, shock and indignation written across their faces. Min had felt a surprising sense of relief, as though the chaos around her had opened a window just wide enough for an opportunity to slip through.

Her application had been weak, vague, and painfully inexperienced—a testament to her untested skills and lack of connections in the field. Anyone else would have rejected her outright.

But not Zenith.

He had looked at the shocked and angry faces, lips curling into a small, amused smirk. Then, in a voice smoother than ice, he had said: "If you can't deal with my attitude, I suggest you leave now...before I piss you off."

One by one, the applicants had stormed out, offended by the bluntness of his words. Those who remained—six of them—were either desperate, fearless, or reckless enough to face him. Min was among them.

Zenith had gone down the line, methodically asking each applicant why they deserved the position and what they could contribute to his already impeccable "team" of engineers. Four applicants had failed miserably, their attempts at flattery and charm crumbling under his incredulous gaze.

Then it came down to Min and a young man far older, far more experienced, whose poise and confidence made her feel very small. Every word he spoke was measured. Every gesture, deliberate. Min had felt herself shrinking inward, shoulders tight, fingers clasped so hard she thought her nails might break.

"And what about you, sweetheart?" Zenith's voice cut through her anxiety, like water poured over a dying hydrangea. "Tell me, what makes you so special?"

She looked up, locking eyes with him. His teal eyes shimmered with a layer of mischief over his supposedly serious exterior. As she raised her head, her hair fell back behind her shoulders, cascading like a dark curtain revealing light she had long searched for.

A silence stretched across the room, taut and almost unbearable. She swallowed, her voice a fragile whisper.

"Nothing."

Zenith's brows arched. "Nothing?"

She nodded, then continued, steadier now, buoyed by the fact that he was actually listening. "I don't have much experience yet," she said, "which means I don't come with habits or expectations you'd have to work around. I learn fast, and I don't waste time pretending I know more than I do."

His gaze stayed on her, assessing. "And what do you think I could possibly need?"

"You said you wanted an assistant."

Zenith let out a surprised laugh, the sound escaping before he could stop it. He scrubbed at his eyes as he caught his breath. "That," he said, smiling despite himself, "is not how most people apply."

Zenith turned toward the older applicant, dismissing him with a single, scornful motion. “You can see yourself out now."

The man's face froze in almost offended shock before it slowly melted away to reveal the seething anger bubbling up from underneath.

"I was the head of the engineering team for Project Minerva! How dare you dismiss me!" His glare followed Min as he stormed from the room, the door slamming shut behind him.

Min looked up at Zenith, uncertain. "So...you want to hire me?"

Zenith rose, his tall frame moving toward her, every motion deliberate, measured, and yet effortlessly graceful. His silver ponytail swayed with each step, the strands catching the light. He stopped just inches from her, his shadow enveloping her like a protective cloak.

"Eighteen hells, sweetheart," he said, stuffing his hands into his pockets, voice suddenly taking on a tone beyond playful teasing. "I want to marry you."

The weight of his words hung in the air, resonant and strange. His eyes softened slightly, but the teasing lilt in his tone never fully vanished. Min's heart pounded loudly in her chest.

* * *

Over the years, that moment had defined them. Not in the simplistic sense of romance, but in the way, Zenith understood her. Not just her skills, work, or ambitions, but her hesitations, fear, desires, and the private ways she compared herself against the world. Zenith saw her. Always. And in return, she had learned to see him, not just the brilliant, infuriatingly handsome engineer, but the man who quietly let others' opinions roll off him like water over polished steel.

She wanted what she felt to be real. She desperately wanted proof that Zenith's presence sparked something in her that no one else could.

Her gaze softened as he adjusted the cuff of his sleeve, his eyes momentarily flicking to her before returning to the conversation with Cronan. The faintest smile tugged at her lips.

He had never stopped calling her sweetheart.

CHAPTER 6

While Min had been observing Zenith, so had he been watching her.

Though he was currently wrapped up in a conversation, if the word wrapped could even apply to the rambling story Cronan was telling him about the family waiting for him back at the main base, the bulk of Zenith's attention never drifted far from Min. His eyes flicked over her every few seconds, tracing the slope of her shoulders, the way she toyed absentmindedly with the loose thread on her sleeve, the tiny crease that formed between her brows whenever she was thinking too hard.

Cronan was married to a guy named Rhei? Uh-huh.

His husband was the sweetest thing to ever live? Amazing.

The Captain missed him very much? Touching. Very touching.

Zenith liked Min? Definitely—

"Wait, what?" Zenith blinked, finally snapping his attention back to the conversation he was allegedly participating in.

Cronan and Kairos exchanged a knowing look. Kairos' wide grin stretched almost comically across her face, her golden eyes sparkling with mischief.

"Aw...look at him," Kairos purred, somehow clasping her four insect arms dramatically beneath her chin. "He's so head-over-heels in love with her, he can't even take his eyes off her."

She immediately began making rapid, chaotic heart-shaped hand signs, her arms folding and unfurling faster than should have been physically possible.

Cronan gave Zenith a hearty pat on the back. "I knew you'd find love someday. Though, frankly, I'm shocked. Your personality certainly didn't help things."

"Oh, please." Zenith rolled his eyes so hard he nearly saw the back of his skull. "We Vaelithari have no need for love or romance or any weak feelings like those. Nor do we pine for it like humans do."

"Mhm." Cronan nodded sympathetically. "Keep telling yourself that, and one day she'll leave you without so much as a glance back."

Zenith sputtered. "I—I don't—she's not—I'm not—"

Kairos leaned forward, smiling like she was witnessing the climax of a juicy soap opera. "You know," she cooed, "a little birdie told me that when you first met her, you asked her to marry you."

Cronan chimed in with a dramatic oohh, and the two began making the teasing sound in unison, like a pair of gossiping parrots, or in their case, a pair of beetles.

Zenith's face turned red so quickly it was impressive. Vaelithari did not blush like humans. The tomato-fication began at the tips of the ears, rolling down the neck before landing across the cheekbones like a setting sun. He looked like someone had just painted a beautiful horizon of embarrassment directly onto him.

"I did no such thing!" Zenith protested, voice cracking. "I-I-I-I said I wanted to marry her, that's all!"

"Oh?" Kairos gasped theatrically. "Love at first sight, it seems!"

The two resumed their ooh-ing with double the intensity. Kairos made a heart with her hands and shoved it mere inches from Zenith's bewildered face.

"It's love, my dear," she declared with absolute, wicked certainty. "Don't fight it."

Zenith turned desperately to Cronan. "Captain, please—"

But the Captain only grinned at him like a proud parent watching his kid fumble through his first crush.

"I'll stop calling you Cronana-banana—Captain!"

"You're doing great, bud."

Zenith opened his mouth to argue.

The lounge doors slid open. Xiangyun entered, walking with a casual bounce to her step and a tray in her hands. One could always tell when she'd been experimenting in the kitchen, rather than in the lab, where she was supposed to be. Her movements carried the air of someone eager—perhaps too eager—to feed unsuspecting victims her newest creation.

She set the tray down. "Plooble calamari, anyone?"

The dish looked harmless enough, vaguely like fried rings of seafood—until one looked closely at the faintly bioluminescent pulses running across the surface of each piece.

Gloop, perched on the counter a few feet away, stared at the tray.

Then they emitted a high-pitched, horrified screech that made Zenith wince.

The little Plooble immediately turned a deep plum color and shivered violently.

Xiangyun burst into laughter. "I'm just joking, Gloop! I would never harm a Plooble!"

Gloop did not appear comforted in the slightest.

In fact, they launched themselves off the counter and propelled their tiny gelatinous body straight toward Min.

Zenith watched with envy as the little octopus alien landed squarely in Min's lap, suction cups sticking to her uniform. She let out a soft laugh, wrapping her arms around the anxious creature.

"Hey there, little guy," Min murmured. She hugged Gloop tight, her voice warm and soothing.

The little octopus purred and began glowing yellow again, their distress fading instantly under her gentle touch.

Zenith had never been so jealous of an octopus in his entire life.

* * *

Juno slurped the last of her instant noodle broth, tilting the cup to drink it like soup. She shoved the empty container aside and stared out the large window on the bridge. Something glimmered in the distance—something big.

"Planet," she muttered.

She blinked. Her cybernetic arm dropped her chopsticks again. Luckily, she had already finished eating.

"Planet!" Juno repeated, louder.

Lance looked up from his corner, where he was carefully examining Xy'vaal's Rubik's cube.

"Huh?" Lance replied, tone flat.

Juno stabbed her finger at the window. "Planet!"

Lance fumbled the cube, caught it, then placed it down with an offended scowl. "I'll call Cronan."

Within minutes, most of the crew had gathered on the bridge. Some still carried half-finished snack packs or drinks from dinner, while others had clearly run here without even finishing their conversations. The air buzzed with low chatter, the scent of Xiangyun's experimental cooking trailing in faint wisps from those who hadn't washed their hands yet.

Zenith leaned against the back wall beside Lance. The cyborg man was still tinkering with the control panel despite

Quori's insistence that he take a break. She had apparently decided that Zenith was the best person to "supervise" Lance while he worked.

Zenith wasn't sure if he should feel insulted or honored.

The only ones missing were Jace and the Medbay staff.

Suddenly, the doors burst open and Jace stumbled in, gasping for air. Sweat dotted his forehead, as he bent over, hands on his knees.

"Apologies," Jace wheezed. "I, uh—ran."

The crew stared at him.

Lance whispered, "Should someone...clap?"

"No," Zenith muttered. "He might collapse. Probably will, whether or not you clap."

Jace slowly straightened, regaining his composure. "Alright—let's go."

Juno, still fiddling with her mechanical arm, tapped a display screen and pulled up the planetary information.

"Behold!" she exclaimed. "Planet!"

The screen showed a shadowy marble suspended in space. Wisps of mist drifted across its surface like luminous fog. Its name flashed on the screen: NOCTILUNE.

"That's eerie," Lance murmured.

Quori pointed toward the oxygen levels and atmospheric pressure. "Pretty dense atmosphere they've got here. But it shouldn't be too different from what we're used to."

Cronan's eyes narrowed. "Strange. This planet wasn't in our projected flight path."

Quori leaned closer, scanning the limited data. She frowned, her brows furrowing deeper with each passing second. Something about the name—Noctilune—tickled a memory she couldn't quite recall. But nothing surfaced. Eventually, she pushed aside her unease and focused on the discussion.

Meanwhile, Min's attention was being split in three separate directions:

Gloop, who was perched on the top of her head, wriggling and adjusting themselves every few seconds.

Psyche, the little girl standing across the room who kept staring at her with unsettling intensity.

Cronan, who was explaining their plan for a scouting team.

Min tried to refocus on Cronan's voice, but Psyche's gaze made the hairs on her arms prickle. The small girl smiled, soft and eerie, and mouthed words that Min recognized instantly.

If you cannot trust anyone, how will you ever know love?

Min flinched and immediately broke eye contact.

Her heart hammered.

That sentence again.

After a few moments, she forced herself to glance toward Zenith.

He caught her watching him.

One eyebrow rose.

Then, with a mildly exasperated expression, he pointed at her head.

Min reached up—barely catching Gloop as the little alien slipped off her hair. She exhaled in relief. Gloop chirped apologetically and burrowed into her arms instead.

Chapter 6

Zenith smirked faintly, crossing his arms.

Min smiled back, grateful, unable to ignore the flutter that stirred again in her stomach.

"We should send a landing team to plant a beacon in order to track our location," Zenith said. Clearly, he had been paying attention to the conversation, unlike Min. "If we could just plant three beacons, we should be able to triangulate our location and find a way back to base."

"How can you be sure that two more planets are gonna pop up?" Juno asked, jumping at the opportunity to poke holes in the Chief Engineer's plans. "How can you be sure that you're not wasting our limited supplies?"

Zenith shrugged. "I can make them out of scrap material. If I don't make something out of the 60 pounds of garbage metal I have building up, you'll be swimming in it pretty soon."

"That's not a bad idea," Cronan agreed, patting the Chief Engineer on the back a little too hard. "I knew hiring you was the right choice."

Now, all that was left was to decide who would be on the landing crew.

"I think Jace would want to go," Liran said, pushing the comms assistant forward.

He shot her a confused look. "I do?"

Xiangyun raised her hand. "I'd like to go."

Jace immediately changed his attitude. "I definitely want to go."

Zenith checked his nails. "And I definitely don't."

Cronan ignored him. "We'll need a medic. I'll grab Wren on the way to the shuttle bay. Zenith, Xiangyun, and Jace, let's go."

The Chief Engineer jumped in surprise, as if electrocuted by the very wall he was leaning on. "Whoa, Captain—you can't just—volunteer me—"

"Yes, I can. Come along now and stop acting like an irritable cat."

"I still need to build the beacon."

Cronan patted him on the head. "Then be quick about it, mister irritable cat."

Zenith's face twisted into the most dramatic grimace imaginable, but he reluctantly followed the others out of the bridge.

"Do you seriously need to drag me into this?" he groaned. "I have better things to do than explore mysterious planets I might possibly lose my life on."

Xiangyun elbowed Zenith brightly. "Come on, it'll be fun!"

For just an instant, the scientist's expression shifted, her previously cheerful face melting back to reveal a sad, hopeless expression.

Sadness.

Pain.

Loss.

It vanished in an instant, but Min caught it, just barely through her peripheral vision. Only because her eyes had been following Zenith, like they always were. Her gaze was inextricably drawn to him.

She watched Xiangyun leave, the barely noticeable slump in her shoulders, the trudging of her steps, and the way the artificial gravity seemed to pull just a little harder on her than everyone else, the truth appearing all the more clear to Min.

She rose slightly, ready to follow Xiangyun, to ask if she was okay, but Lance stopped her.

"Come on, dude. She's long gone." Lance's voice had a layer of sadness Min wasn't used to hearing from him. He tossed her a smile.

"But she's—"

"Come on, Min." Lance grew serious. "She's none of your business. Leave the comforting to Jace."

"Okay..." Min backed off, her eyes trailing after the scientist's disappearing figure. "Dude, chill."

* * *

My dear Xiangyun,

I don't think we're a good fit anymore. I know you only wanted to be with me because it was your parents' last wish, but now that they're gone, I think it would be best for both of us to be free now.

On another note, I've found someone I can love with my entire heart. Would you mind if I kept the inheritance your parents so kindly left to me? You're going on that space exploration mission anyways, so you won't be needing it anytime soon.

Your fiancé

—from Xiangyun's personal belongings

CHAPTER 7

After the crew meeting, Min found Zenith tinkering away in a corner of the Engine Room. A large pile of scrap material towered over him like an unconquerable mountain, his mission to create three beacons out of what he had seemed equally impossible. In one hand, he held a S16 model of the alliance-sanctioned soldering pen.

Of course, he had made some minor adjustments to it, according to his unique personal tastes. The monstrosity of a soldering pen that he was holding at the moment was definitely not alliance sanctioned.

Min walked up behind him, stealing a look over his shoulder at what he was working on before spotting a nearby ledge on the wall and pushing herself up to sit on it.

She watched Zenith mess around with the reject parts for fifteen minutes, until finally, he finished, triumphantly holding up the basketball-shaped beacon with a flat base. A thin antenna poked up from what appeared to be the top of the ball, a small teal light flashing cheerfully, its light reflected in Zenith's eyes.

He looked up at Min. "Do you like it?"

She nodded. "It's nice."

Zenith set the beacon down on the table. "I don't think nice is enough." He let out a mock pout.

Min rolled her eyes. She slid herself onto the edge of the ledge, pushing herself off it, dropping smoothly to the ground.

Min glanced at the finished beacon. "I guess it's a little better than nice."

Zenith leaned back against the table. He ran a hand through his hair, hooking a finger into the rubber band holding his ponytail together, and pulled, releasing his long silver hair to cascade down his back in a waterfall of starlight.

"That's not enough either."

"Oh, come on, Zenith. You know it's perfect..."

Just like you. The unfinished end of her sentence floated away in her mind, her heart too desperate for a confession, yet too cowardly to voice it.

"Of course it is—"

Before Zenith could finish, Min wrapped her arms around Zenith, leaning into him, her long hair becoming an extension of the silver waterfall flowing from his head, the strands of their hair tangling together as if preparing for a final embrace.

Zenith froze. "Why are you acting like this? What's wrong?"

"Don't die. Please."

He let out a relieved laugh. "It's not that bad. I'm just taking a short stroll on a completely foreign planet not recorded on the alliance database with a possibly explosive beacon I built in fifteen minutes out of scrap parts because our poor ship's lost." He paused. "Oh, that sounds very bad."

Zenith looked down at Min, and smirked.

"I bet the UV radiation is horrible too. Oh, the terrible things it's gonna do to my porcelain skin."

She giggled. "Sunscreen exists, you know?"

"I don't like the texture."

Min poked him in the chest. "Of course you wouldn't."

Zenith smiled. "I'm not going to die."

* * *

Stepping foot on Noctilune was like walking into a dream. A dream spun from neon threads, humming engines, and the kind of impossible geometry that humans would've once called "futuristic" before the galaxy redefined the word.

A cool wind swept across the landing zone, carrying with it the faint metallic tang of ionized minerals. Beneath the crew, the planet's surface was a strange purple-brown shade, shifting like oil on water whenever the light touched it. The ground gave way slightly underfoot. The sand was grainy, and almost warm.

High above them, towers rose from a deep gorge of elegant spirals of metal and glass, glowing with soft pulses of electric blue. Floating walkways connected them like strands of a web. Flying vehicles glided between the structures in complete silence, distinctly missing that telltale hum of engines. Lights trailed behind them in a dozen iridescent colors.

"This place looks like the cities in those vintage sci-fi movies!" Wren blurted, eyes wide as he spun in a full circle. "The ones with the retro commercials and the bad robot costumes. It's like—like someone turned my childhood poster into a real place!"

Xiangyun couldn't help a small smile. Her heart felt heavy, weighted with everything she'd been carrying, but Wren's excitement tugged her upward just a bit, like gravity had eased for a moment. "Yeah," she murmured. "It's...super cool."

"Yun'er." Jace's voice was gentle, almost careful. "Are you feeling alright?"

His brows knotted together the way they only did when he was worried—when he wasn't sure what to do with his hands, or his voice, or the fact that he genuinely cared too much for everyone on Horizon-2. Especially Xiangyun.

She didn't look at him. Didn't trust herself to. Her reflection in his nanotech helmet—the helmet that everyone was wearing—would just show a stranger anyway.

"...yeah. I'm fine."

Jace didn't believe her. She knew he didn't.

He also didn't push.

The group walked the last stretch of the rocky slope toward the shimmering gate marking the entrance to the alien city. Huge metal arches, twisted into shapes that reminded Wren of dragon spines, towered over the walkway, etched with glowing runes that pulsed in rhythmic waves.

As the crew approached, three tall figures stepped forward from the shadow beneath the arch.

Humanoid.

But wrong.

Pale, grayish skin stretched taut over long limbs. Their eyes were pools of absolute crimson, no whites, no pupils, just crimson, like lit coals. Their hair was black and slick, hanging like liquid shadow down their backs. And when they opened their mouths...

Two rows of pointed, glistening teeth greeted them.

The aliens spoke in perfect harmony, their voices blending into a single eerie chord, like organ pipes echoing in some enormous cathedral.

"We are the Stryx. Welcome to Noctilune, travelers."

Wren leaned sideways until his shoulder bumped Jace's. "Is it just me," he whispered, "or do they look like vampires?"

Jace didn't answer. His gaze flickered uneasily across the Stryx—their posture, the synchronized dilation of their crimson eyes, the faint, almost imperceptible distortion in the air around them.

Zenith, however, spoke in a low mutter meant only for Cronan. "How convenient that they speak flawless Standard," he said, suspicions curling each word like smoke. "Too convenient."

The Captain subtly nudged his arm. "Don't start trouble. We

just landed."

"I don't start trouble," Zenith replied. "I reveal it."

In reality, he was just cranky because he had to carry the stupid beacon.

But he said nothing further.

The Stryx bowed smoothly, oddly synchronizing like an earth pop boy band, motioning for the crew to follow them through the massive gates.

* * *

Stepping past the archway felt like slipping into a different world entirely.

The interior of the gorge-city swelled open into a breathtaking expanse—tower after tower, each built from glowing alloys and prismatic glass that refracted the city lights into ceaseless cascades of color. Gardens floated midair in suspended platforms, their flowers emitting soft luminescence. Delicate orbs of drifting light hovered lazily through the streets like fireflies made of neon.

Everything was beautiful. Too beautiful.

Jace slowed, taking it in with hesitant admiration.

Wren on the other hand, practically vibrated with glee.

"Oh my stars," he squeaked. "Is that a building shaped like a treble clef? And that one—look, it's like a giant crystalline flower! I want to live here forever."

"And here I thought you hated overly designed architecture," Zenith teased.

"I hate ugly overly designed architecture," Wren corrected. "This is ART."

Zenith snorted.

The Stryx slid ahead of them, gliding rather than walking. Their long coats, woven from fiber the color of midnight, swished behind them like bat wings.

"Our city is a sanctuary," one said, still in that eerie voice. "A refuge from sorrow. From pain. From the burdens of memory."

"Sounds wonderful." Zenith rolled his eyes. The beacon in his arms seemed to grow heavier by the minute.

Xiangyun barely heard him. Her eyes were fixed on the world before her, on the impossible glow of the floating platforms, the serene soundscape of soft chimes drifting from no visible source, and the gentle warmth that seemed to seep into her bones with every breath she took.

Peace.

She hadn't felt peace in months.

Not since the call from the hospital. Not since the final, cruel argument with her fiancé. Not since she'd stood alone in a tiny apartment surrounded by memories of which she couldn't let go and belongings she couldn't drop.

Here, the ache in her chest finally dulled.

That was dangerous, but she couldn't make herself care.

* * *

The group was led through a market square, where stalls crafted from shimmering metal displayed arrays of alien foods, glowing fruits, and ornaments that caught the light in mesmerizing ways. The air smelled faintly of jasmine and warm sugar.

From beneath one of the stalls, a creature scuttled out.

Then another.

Then several.

The creatures were small—barely reaching Wren's knee—fluffy and iridescent, like living hummingbirds made of starlight. Their long ears twitched rapidly, and their multiple eyes blinked out of sync. The moment they spotted the crew, they emitted chirping noises, hopping excitedly.

"Awwww," Wren gasped. "They're adorable! What are they?"

The Stryx answered without turning. "Etoilies. House companions. Pets. Harmless."

One of the Etoilies bounded up to Cronan and immediately latched onto the hem of his pant leg, gnawing on the fabric with tiny needle-teeth.

"Uh—hey—hey, buddy—!"

Jace bent down and pried the creature off with the clumsy movement of someone unaccustomed to furry companions.

The Etoilie immediately latched onto his glove instead.

"It's like a cosmic chinchilla," Wren said, delighted.

"It's eating my equipment." Jace smiled awkwardly.

The Stryx turned slightly. "A minor inconvenience. They enjoy chewing. We...discourage them from interacting with visitors."

He said this just as a nearby Etoilie launched itself at Zenith's chest.

Cronan snorted.

Jace sighed.

The creature latched on harder as Zenith tried to pry it off. Finally, after a terrible struggle, the Etoilie had been detached, claws bloody with Vaelithari blood.

Meanwhile, Xiangyun watched the little creatures with soft eyes. She crouched, extending a gentle hand. One Etoilie drifted closer, sniffing her palm before curling into it like a newborn star.

The warmth it radiated seeped into her fingers.

She didn't want to let go.

* * *

The deeper they walked, the more the city shimmered. The buildings began to ripple, just slightly, like reflections on water. The neon lights seemed to pulse in rhythm with the crew's heartbeats.

Zenith stopped walking. His arms were burning from carrying the beacon, which, at the present moment, felt twice as heavy as it did when he first disembarked from the shuttle. Something was off.

"Captain," he said quietly. "Look."

Cronan, who had been trying very hard to appear relaxed, followed Zenith's gaze.

One of the towers in the distance flickered, its edges blurring for a split second, like a glitch in a hologram.

Then it stabilized.

"An illusion?" Cronan whispered.

"Or something worse," Zenith replied.

Wren swallowed. "Maybe one of their power grids is malfunctioning?"

"No." Zenith's voice hardened. "The distortion wasn't mechanical. It was neurological."

Jace blinked. "Meaning...?"

"Meaning it didn't glitch in reality," Zenith said. "It glitched in our perception of it."

Xiangyun didn't hear the conversation.

Or perhaps she did and chose not to react, because at that moment, the tower seemed perfect again. The lights shimmered like stars caught in crystal.

Maybe I'm imagining things, she told herself. Maybe it's just fatigue.

Or maybe she didn't care.

Not when this place finally made her feel at ease.

* * *

The Stryx guided them into a vast hall carved directly into the stone of the gorge wall. Translucent curtains of light drifted from the ceiling like bioluminescent waterfalls.

"This is our reception chamber," the Stryx intoned. "You may rest here. Dine. Explore. We offer peace, freedom from suffering."

Zenith's jaw clenched. "You keep saying that."

"Because it is what all travelers desire most."

Zenith was about to argue when Xiangyun stepped forward.

"Can I explore on my own?"

Jace looked up sharply. "Yun'er—"

"I just want to look around. I'll stay nearby."

Cronan hesitated, but her expression—peaceful for the first time since they left the ship—disarmed him.

"Stay within sight of the plaza," he ordered gently. "Don't

wander too far."

She nodded.

But as she walked away, the soft glow of the city seemed to fold around her— pulling her in deeper.

* * *

Zenith paced the chamber. He had set his makeshift beacon down in one of the corners of the room, hidden from view unless someone went looking for it. The system was still booting up, so the crew had no choice but to wait until it finished before leaving. Zenith tapped his foot.

"I don't like this. I don't like any of this."

Jace stood up. "We should find Xiangyun."

Wren nodded. "The sooner we leave this place, the better."

Zenith approached Cronan. "Captain, I have a bad feeling."

Cronan's smile was thin. "Me too."

The beacon finished booting up. They stepped out into the city again.

And the illusion, for a moment, dropped.

It was subtle, so subtle that if Zenith hadn't been watching, it would've gone unnoticed. For a split second, the flowing gardens flickered into shriveled vines. The towers became cracked stone pillars. The floating lights turned into drifting spores.

Then everything snapped back to perfection.

"What—what was that?" Wren whispered, voice trembling.

Zenith answered first.

"A feeding ground."

Wren's stomach dropped. "What...what do they feed on?"

Zenith didn't answer. He didn't have to.

Because up ahead, at the far end of the plaza, a figure stood in front of a mirror-like panel embedded in a wall.

Xiangyun.

She was staring at the panel with rapt attention.

The reflection it showed was not what stood before it.

It showed Xiangyun happy.

Whole.

Her parents standing behind her.

Smiling. Alive.

Her fiancé's arms around her shoulders.

The future she was supposed to have.

"Yun'er," Jace breathed.

Xiangyun's eyes were glassy, childlike.

"It's beautiful," she whispered, barely audible. "They said...they said I could stay. That I don't have to be hurt anymore."

Jace stepped closer. "Yun'er, please. It isn't real."

"It feels real."

"That's because they're making it feel real," Zenith snapped. "It's a trap. They drain you until there's nothing left."

Her eyes were shimmering unnaturally, reflecting the city lights in a way that made her pupils look like molten silver.

"I don't wanna go back," she whispered. Her voice broke.

"Back there, I'm alone." She stabbed a finger into Jace's chest, prompting him to stumble backwards. "Back there, there's nothing left for me. Here...here I can rest."

Cronan's voice was quiet, as if speaking too loudly would shatter something fragile. "Xiangyun...you have us."

Tears filled her eyes.

But she didn't step away from the panel.

Behind her, shadows were gathering. Shadows with glowing red eyes.

The Stryx.

"We cannot allow her to leave," the Stryx said calmly. "She is already connected to the Dreamstream."

"Disconnect her," Zenith hissed.

"That is not possible."

Jace moved forward. "Like hell it isn't—"

The Stryx blocked him instantly, crimson eyes flaring.

"She made her choice."

"She's not thinking clearly!" Wren shouted.

"She is thinking more clearly than ever," the Stryx corrected. "She sees the truth. Pain is unnecessary. Memories are unnecessary. We offer peace. Eternal, blissful peace."

Zenith stepped in front of Wren, who was trembling under the horrifying red gaze of the creatures. "You offer death."

"We offer release."

Wren tugged Zenith back. "We need a plan. We can't fight them all."

Jace swallowed hard. "Yun'er. Please. I can grieve with you—for you. You don't have to do it alone."

Xiangyun smiled softly.

It was the saddest smile Jace had ever seen.

"I'm tired," she whispered, barely loud enough for him to hear. "So, so tired."

Then she turned fully toward the panel and placed her hand upon it.

The city lights brightened.

The illusion sharpened.

The Stryx stepped toward her with slow, reverent grace.

"No!" Jace lunged forward—

A Stryx slammed him back with inhuman strength.

Wren screamed. Cronan grabbed him. Zenith surged forward only for three more Stryx to seize him by the arms.

Cronan shouted orders the city swallowed.

Xiangyun's body stiffened as the panel radiated sickly light. Her face relaxed, peaceful, serene, as though drifting into sleep.

Then her skin began to pale.

Then gray.

Then thin.

Her cheeks sank sharply.

Her hair dulled and fell against her shriveling shoulders.

Her fingers curled inward like dying petals.

Chapter 7

"YUN'ER!" Jace's voice cracked, raw with agony.

The Stryx did not look away. Did not waver.

They watched with clinical serenity as Xiangyun's life force was drawn from her, an invisible stream of shimmering light flowing from her chest into the panel.

Her body dried rapidly, collapsing inward like grapes left in the sun.

Her eyes, once dark and warm and full of gentle sorrow, hollowed into empty sockets.

Jace sobbed.

Wren clung to Zenith.

Cronan stood frozen, horror carved into every feature.

The light flickered.

The last of Xiangyun's glow vanished.

And her husk—dry, wrinkled, weightless—crumpled to the floor like a dead leaf.

A memory turned to dust.

The moment was interrupted by the sound of two gamma-blasters charging up, the slow vibrating sound menacing in its own way. Cronan and Zenith, back-to-back, blaster barrels locked onto their targets.

The Stryx backed away, their eyes dimming.

"She is at peace now," they said softly.

"How about I give you a taste of your so-called 'peace?'" Zenith said, index finger hovering over the trigger.

"You cannot kill us. We are the Stryx. We cannot die."

Zenith's voice was ice. "If I ever return to this planet, I will burn your illusions to ash."

The Stryx grinned, sharp teeth gleaming in the renewed light of the illusion. "You're welcome to try...but we won't be seeing each other again."

The crew lifted Jace—shaking, broken—off the ground and pulled him away from Xiangyun's lifeless form. They left the city in silence, illusions glimmering around them, mocking—whispering promises Xiangyun had believed.

The shuttle took off without ceremony.

No one spoke.

Not until the world below was a shrinking violet smudge in the darkness and the Horizon-2 could be seen approaching rapidly.

Then, quietly, Jace whispered into the silent cabin: "...I told her she wasn't alone."

Zenith's jaw tightened.

Wren cried softly in his arms.

Cronan stared straight ahead, expression unreadable.

The stars stretched before them, cold, distant, unchanging.

And behind them, on the dream-planet of Noctilune, Xiangyun slept forever.

CHAPTER 8

"You're kidding me."

Zenith's voice ricocheted through the entire room, sharp, incredulous, and vibrating with that particular timbre he only used when reality personally offended him.

He and Min stood shoulder to shoulder, framed by the harsh white glow of the diagnostics panel overhead. The engine room was usually a symphony of ordered chaos—vibrating metal, humming conduits, the warm metallic scent of coolant circulating through the floor grate. But now a very different scent greeted them: melted insulation and...was that drool?

Because sitting innocently inside the open electrical closet, cheeks puffed out and blue-black fur sticking up like it had been electrocuted, was a tiny Etoilie. Its big silver eyes blinked at them with the soft glow of bioluminescence.

The heating cord for the right wing was dangling from its mouth in shreds.

Min pressed her palms together as if praying for patience.

Zenith sighed. "Of course it's an Etoilie. Of all the creatures that could've snuck onto the ship."

The creature let out a chirring squeak. It was almost apologetic.

Almost.

Zenith crouched, his expression a slow-building storm. "Do you have any idea," he said, voice lowering dangerously, "how long it took me to wire this system after that one—" he jabbed an accusatory finger in Min's direction. "—messed with the breakers last month? Weeks. Weeks, you tiny little carpet stain."

The Etoilie blinked again.

It smiled.

Puppy-dog eyes.

Zenith's left eye twitched. "I'm throwing you out."

"Zenith—wait—" Min started, stepping forward as Zenith reached in with two long, elegant fingers, pinching the creature by the scruff of its neck, or what counted as its neck. It wriggled, squeaked, tried to cling to the metal panel with suction-like paws. Uselessly.

"Nope. No sympathy points," Zenith declared. "You gnawed through a heating cord. I don't even gnaw through heating cords, and I have fangs."

"You absolutely do not," Min muttered.

Zenith ignored that.

He marched to the trash chute like a man walking to a guillotine, except he was the executioner and the Etoilie was the condemned. His footsteps thudded across the grating. He slapped open the chute door with dramatic flair.

The Etoilie whined, long and pitiful.

Min winced. "Zenith—maybe don't—"

"Goodbye," Zenith said. Then, with theatrical precision, he stuffed the Etoilie inside and stabbed the ejection button with his middle finger.

FWOOMP.

The far end of the trash chute opened, and the Etoilie disappeared into the sprawling, glittering darkness of space.

Silence.

Then Zenith hissed sharply and shook his hand. "Ow. I think I jammed my finger."

Chapter 8

Min stared. "Uh-huh." She crossed her arms. "You didn't have to throw it off the ship."

"It chewed a structural heating cable, sweetheart. Either it leaves or we freeze."

"Still."

Zenith massaged his abused finger. "We should tell Cronan before he finds out the fun way, like, oh I don't know—approaching a frozen wing mid-flight."

Min rolled her eyes and tapped her comms watch, punching in the Captain's line. "I wonder whose fault this was," she muttered.

Zenith pressed a hand to his heart. "Sweetheart, you wound me."

"Yeah, well, at least I'm not the one throwing wildlife out of airlocks."

"Trash chute," Zenith corrected. "Totally different."

The screen flickered. Cronan appeared, squinting, sweaty, and definitely wincing.

"That's Medbay in the background," Min said, narrowing her eyes.

Cronan sighed. "Min! What's up?"

"We had a stowaway," Min said. "It chewed through the right wing heating cord."

"Well...that's unfortunate." He yelped suddenly. "Ow! Kairos—gentle!"

"You're at Medbay," Min said flatly.

"Yes," Cronan admitted, flinching again. "Ow! Stop poking me!"

Zenith stiffened.

Min slowly turned. "Zenith...are you hurt?"

His hands flew up to cover his torso. "Define 'hurt.'"

"Zenith," Cronan said helpfully, "got absolutely wrecked by one of the Etoilies when we were exploring the Noctilune marketplace. Big gash, bleeding everywhere—"

"Captain," Zenith warned, "I will personally reassemble your bed so it collapses the second you sit on it."

Cronan ignored him. "Anyway, Kairos says he needs to come in for stitches and stuff. So, uh, good luck! Fix the heating cord whenever. Or don't. We don't really need the right wing, probably."

The line cut.

"Sweetheart—" Zenith started.

Min took a slow, deep breath. "Medbay. Now."

Zenith didn't argue.

* * *

Medbay was dim and quiet when they entered. The overhead lights had been turned down—Kairos claimed it reduced patient anxiety, but Zenith insisted it made him look like a horror movie villain.

“A hot horror movie villain,” was what Wren had said.

Kairos looked up the moment the door slid open. "Zenith. Shirt off."

Zenith recoiled like the doctor had brandished a weapon. "I'm fine. Really. It looks worse than—"

Kairos lifted a sterilizing pad with tweezers. "Shirt. Off."

Chapter 8

Zenith looked at Min.

Min raised a brow.

He sighed dramatically and gingerly peeled off his shirt. Under the harsh examination lights, the injuries were...bad. Two long gashes carved diagonally across his chest, already bruising purple. His forearms bore teeth marks, jagged and ugly, still slightly swollen.

Min sucked in a quiet breath.

Zenith glanced sideways at her, catching the flash of worry in her expression, and for once, he said nothing cocky.

Kairos grabbed the shirt and tossed it at Min. She was not prepared to be assaulted by a clothing garment. She caught it—barely—right as it slipped over her face.

It smelled faintly of jasmine.

And smoke.

And Zenith.

"Dang," she muttered before she could stop herself. "You smell nice."

Zenith's smirk was instant. "I'm sure I look even better, sweetheart."

Min nearly dropped the shirt again. She spun around so fast she nearly knocked into a supply cart. "I-I'm checking the announcement stream," she mumbled, grabbing a tablet just to have something to hold.

Kairos cleaned Zenith's wounds with ruthless efficiency. Zenith hissed, winced, swore in three languages Min didn't recognize, and once even tried to crawl backwards off the cot.

"Unless you're secretly a lizard," Kairos said, "you don't regenerate. Hold still."

"You're sadistic," Zenith grumbled.

"You bite," Kairos said calmly. "So we're even."

It took nearly ten minutes, by which point Min's blush had cooled and Zenith looked significantly less like someone who had fought a small, angry bear.

Then Min spoke.

"Oh."

Zenith straightened. "What's wrong?"

She turned the tablet for both him and Kairos to see.

Cronan's most recent announcement scrolled across the screen:

"Due to temporary heating failure in the right wing, all junior crew members assigned to the wing will bunk with their senior officers until repairs can be completed."

Zenith blinked.

Then a slow, wicked smile curled his lips. "Well, sweetheart. Looks like you'll be seeing a lot more of me."

His bare chest brushed her back as he reached over her shoulder to tap the notification.

Min practically combusted.

Zenith pulled his shirt back on with exaggerated care—making sure not to disturb the gemstone set in his forehead—then sauntered out of Medbay like hadn't just sent her brain spiraling into the sun.

Min sighed, staring at the door he left through.

Then someone tapped her shoulder.

She nearly jumped out of her skin.

Turning, she found a girl, small, ethereal, with pale brunette curls and eyes the cold green of algae under ice.

Psyche.

She smiled, soft as a knife sliding under skin. "Isn't this a lovely arrangement?" she asked sweetly.

"Uh...what?"

Psyche tilted her head. "Better savor it before it's all gone."

Then she stepped through the Medbay doors and vanished into the corridor without another sound.

Min stared after her, a pit forming in her stomach.

Even the quiet hum of the Medbay felt suddenly too loud.

* * *

The hallway lights flickered as Min walked back toward her cabin—her *shared* cabin—with a brain full of too many emotions and not nearly enough instructions for what to do with them.

Zenith was already there, leaning against the door, poking at his bandages. The golden glow of the torch-lamp he had installed in the wall outside his room cast warm light across his features, softening the sharp lines of his face.

He looked up as Min approached.

"I'm fine, see?" He held up his arms for her to see. "Kairos is overdramatic. A little blood never killed anyone."

"It could've killed you."

He paused.

Then he smirked and cocked his head. "Worried about me?"

She turned away just in time so he wouldn't see her blush. "I just don't want to lose my boss. That would make my job harder."

"Mhm," he said, unconvinced.

Min hesitated, then repeated Psyche's words aloud before she could stop herself. "Zenith? Do you think everything's about to go wrong?"

Zenith's expression shifted, playfulness fading, seriousness rising in its place. "Why?"

"Psyche said...this, all of this, is going to disappear."

Zenith stared.

Then he huffed, rolling his eyes. "Min, she's twelve. And possibly psychic, but mostly twelve."

"That doesn't make me feel better," Min muttered.

Zenith walked up to her, sliding his arms underneath hers, fitting perfectly into the hug like a puzzle piece that should've been there all along. "If everything goes to hell, sweetheart, I promise I'll save you first."

She blinked at him.

He winked.

Of course he winked.

Her face heated so fast she thought she might combust. "Goodnight," she squeaked, sliding open the door.

Zenith laughed softly.

A warm, tired, genuine sound.

* * *

She is perfect. Intelligent. Beautiful. Invincible.

Chapter 8

Everything I set out to create with Project Minerva. Her name will be Minerva like the goddess of wisdom and war. She is the innovation the world has been waiting for, and I am the one who made her. Eros is nothing. I am her true creator.

I am God.

—from Dr. Lysander Cale's notes about Project Minerva

CHAPTER 9

Zenith's room was only moderately less messy than the engine room, which was an achievement, considering that the engine room was a near-apocalyptic maze of loose wires, suspicious scorch marks, and half-assembled devices Zenith insisted were "in progress." Still, it took Min less than a second to form her verdict on his living space.

This room was disgusting.

Neglected piles of uniforms slumped like defeated soldiers in lopsided stacks around the room. Undergarments—clean? used? unclassifiable?—lay half-buried under spare gloves, wrenches, data pads, and a few stray ration bars whose expiration labels had faded to guesswork. The lighting panel above flickered occasionally, as if embarrassed to illuminate the chaos.

The walls were a glaring white, the sterile type that really only made the mess stand out more, as though mocking him for every item out of place.

Min stood in the doorway, taking it all in.

How did he live like this?

Zenith, of course, didn't notice or care. He stepped past her, nudging a mountain of uniforms aside with his foot so he could shut the door.

"There," he said, as if he had done something impressive. "Home sweet home."

Min pressed a hand to her forehead. "Zenith..."

"I know, I know." He gestured vaguely toward the clutter. "You can put your bag anywhere."

"Anywhere?" Her gaze traveled across the floor. She wasn't

certain if the "floor" was even visible. There were geological layers of clothing in some places. Anthropologists could have studied them.

Zenith noticed her hesitation and rolled his eyes. "Sweetheart, it's not that bad."

"It's a biohazard."

He scoffed dramatically. "Everything on this ship is a biohazard. That's the charm."

Min didn't dignify that with a reply. Instead, she stepped cautiously over a heap of jumpsuits, trying not to step on anything that might be alive, sentient, or contagious. To her relief, there was one redeeming feature in the disaster zone.

Zenith had made his bed.

Perfectly. The sheets were tucked with military precision, the blanket smoothed without a single wrinkle, each pillow aligned with almost obsessive symmetry. For a moment Min wondered if Zenith had made it, or if someone else had stepped in out of pity.

She approached the bed and sat carefully at the edge, grateful for a surface not constructed out of old clothing and despair.

The rest of the room was...more organized than she'd first thought. Hidden under the chaos was evidence of an oddly meticulous mind. A tall floor-to-ceiling shelf consumed one wall, filled with books, artifacts, old components, crystalline vials of fluorescent liquids, and half-disassembled gadgets. The books, incredibly, were arranged alphabetically by author's last name.

Min blinked.

She looked up. A large wall-mounted, holographic screen was pulled up above his desk, currently displaying a rotating 3D model of what appeared to be an engine manifold so complex it looked like a piece of modern art. The desk had been shoved flush against the bed, clearly acting as a hybrid workbench and nightstand, a combination only someone like Zenith would consider practical.

He had also left a mug there, half filled with something that had congealed into a suspicious paste. She eyed it with alarm before forcing herself to look away.

"Cozy, right?" Zenith said.

Min slowly backed up towards the door, exhaling slowly. "Sure."

If "cozy" meant "potential category-five disaster zone."

She dropped her duffel bag beside the door, then navigated toward the bed again, weaving through the piles until she successfully reached it. It felt like crossing a minefield.

By the time she sat, exhaustion finally hit her. The entire day crashed over her—the discovery of Noctilune, watching the holographic recap, Xiangyun's unsettling behavior, her horrifying end.

Memories rose unbidden: Xiangyun's bright smile, the brittle cracks beneath it, the way her final minutes had twisted into something grotesque and agonizing.

Min sniffled.

It was too much.

She sank further into the bed.

"I'm sleeping on the bed," she said suddenly, her voice flat with the finality of someone who could not handle one more problem in her life. "You can sleep on the floor."

Zenith froze mid-step.

"...sweetheart." He approached, placing his hands on the mattress near her legs, leaning over her. The subtle dip of the bedding under his weight tilted her slightly toward him. His eyes, cold and sharp as ice, bore down on her with heat and intensity that made her pulse skip.

"This is my room."

Min gulped and forcibly blinked away the rather scandalous images her exhausted brain conjured. "And I need my beauty sleep."

Zenith arched an eyebrow. "And what about me?"

"You're handsome enough. You don't need it."

"Rude."

"No." She crossed her arms, lips flattening into a line. "Realistic."

Zenith let out a soft, breathy laugh. Something warm flickered in his eyes before he stepped back, running slender fingers through his long, silky hair. The motion made the smooth strands cascade across his shoulders and shimmer under the harsh white lights.

"If I'd known that you'd end up being so disagreeable," he sighed dramatically, "I wouldn't have hired you."

She shot him a glare sharp enough to cut sheet metal.

Zenith raised both hands in surrender. "Alright, alright, sweetheart. You win."

He backed away from the bed with the defeated slump of a man whose dignity had been confiscated, then lowered himself grudgingly onto the floor with a groan.

Min didn't answer. She simply turned to the wall, pulling the blanket up to her chin.

Silence slowly filled the room.

Zenith shifted once, then twice, then a third time. He could not get comfortable on the floor. The hard metal grated against his shoulder blades. He tugged his ponytail out and tried coiling it under his head like a makeshift cushion. That only worked until it tugged painfully at his scalp.

Min's breathing signaled she was already slipping into sleep.

For a while, he sat upright, elbows on his knees, hands fidgeting with something invisible. The memory of Xiangyun's final moments flickered through his mind like a corrupted video feed. Her desperation. Her cracked, collapsing face. The way she had crumpled as she lost everything that made her human.

Zenith swallowed hard.

He pulled out something from under a mound of clothes.

A thin, teal cord—the replacement heating cable for the destroyed wire system.

He'd known where it was all along.

He stared down at it, turning it slowly between his fingers.

His own voice whispered across his thoughts: Zenith, what are you doing? You're ridiculous. Absolutely, pathetically ridiculous.

The cable bent, smiling up at him.

He knew exactly what he'd done. Exactly what it meant.

He shouldn't have hidden it. He shouldn't have sabotaged the repair schedule by omission. He shouldn't have created the perfect excuse for Min to stay near him—for days, maybe longer.

He wasn't supposed to be like this.

Vaelithari didn't get attached. They didn't form bonds. They didn't pine, or yearn, or—

He exhaled sharply, rubbing his forehead with the heel of his palm.

"Get it together," he muttered.

But the words had no weight.

With a small groan, Zenith pushed himself to his feet. He crossed to his tall bookshelf and slid the cord behind a thick, dusty textbook on gravitational field manipulation.

Out of sight. Out of mind. Out of reach.

He turned back toward the bed.

Min lay there, breathing slow and rhythmic, lashes resting like fragile brushstrokes against her cheeks. Her brow was relaxed for once, no tension, no guarded expression. Just peaceful stillness.

It drew him in like gravity.

He approached without realizing he was doing it. Stood beside the bed. Then sat lightly on its edge.

His posture was tight, controlled, like he was trying to restrain himself from doing something stupid. Or worse, something sincere.

A stray strand of her hair had fallen across her cheek.

Zenith reached out.

His fingers brushed it gently back behind her ear.

The moment his skin touched hers, something cold rippled along his fingertips.

Not normal cold. Not human cold.

It was the chill of polished stone, of something carved with unnatural precision.

His breath stilled.

He examined her face more closely—her symmetry, the perfection of her features. The unnerving stillness in her sleep. Too still. Too quiet.

Yet he didn't pull away.

Something in him whispered that she was dangerous. Something else whispered that she was precious.

He withdrew his hand.

Stop being insane. Nothing is wrong with her.

He stood abruptly, stepping away from the bed as if retreating from the edge of a cliff.

He wasn't supposed to be like this.

Vaelithari didn't fall in love.

They didn't crave comfort.

They didn't curl up next to someone like some abandoned kitten desperate for warmth.

Yet.

Minutes later, as exhaustion wore away the last of his restraint, Zenith quietly crawled onto the bed—careful, careful, careful—to not wake her.

He curled up on top of the blanket beside her, not touching but near enough to breathe easier.

And for the first time since he lost his best friend, he slept without nightmares.

* * *

Outside the room, in the dim, quiet hallway, a shadow

shifted.

Psyche pressed her ear to the door, listening with rapt fascination. When she finally leaned back, a small grin slithered across her lips—sharp, knowing, far beyond her apparent age.

"Things are getting interesting," she whispered, to no one in particular.

Her bare feet padded against the floor as she tiptoed away. Silent as a ghost. Swift as a thought. There one moment, gone the next.

The ship slept.

And in its silence, something dark began to stir.

CHAPTER 10

Zenith was violently ripped from his pleasant dreams by a bloodcurdling scream right next to his ear. He jolted awake like a malfunctioning android. The world spun, cold metal slammed into his hip, and he found himself sprawled on the floor, staring up at the ceiling. His tailbone throbbed with the kind of pain he wasn't awake enough to process.

"Well good morning to you too," he grumbled, his voice thick with sleep. He blinked slowly, trying to peel his eyelids apart. "Is this some exotic expression of greeting, or were you attempting to make me deaf in one ear?

Min sat rigidly on the bed, clutching the blanket around herself like a shield against an intruder. Her hair stuck up in disheveled tufts, her face burning a bright red that had nothing to do with temperature and everything to do with mortification.

Upon hearing his snark, she grabbed the pillow that had been peacefully resting near her shoulder, lifted it with both hands, and hurled it directly at his head with surprising force.

It hit him with a muted whump, accompanied by a dignified grunt of pain.

"Ow."

Zenith rubbed the side of his cheek, offended that a pillow could hurt that much.

"You—" Min sputtered, pointing an accusatory finger but unable to manage a coherent sentence, "you—why were you—"

Zenith blinked once. Twice. Then his lips curled slowly, the corners lifting in a shamelessly self-satisfied grin.

"Sweetheart...this is my room. I thought we'd been over this already."

Min opened her mouth, then closed it. Then opened it again. Nothing but indignant air came out. Her eyes darted everywhere except at him.

Zenith took advantage of her speechlessness and scooted closer, resting his forearms on the mattress edge like a cat settling in to watch a show.

"Besides, the floor was too cold," he said casually, shrugging one shoulder. "So, I didn't feel like sleeping on it anymore."

"You—" Min buried her face into the blanket with a groan somewhere between frustration and despair. "Just—don't do it again."

"Oh, I'll do what I want, sweetheart." His tone was light, playful. Infuriating.

"That's not—Zenith—!" She flailed a hand toward him.

His smirk deepened. "See? You do like saying my name in the morning."

She almost died on the spot.

Before she could summon the strength or courage to retaliate further, her comms watch beeped loudly—the shrill tone bouncing off the walls. She fumbled with it, tapping the display with the grace of someone trying very hard not to combust.

Cronan's voice filled the cramped room.

"My sincerest apologies if I'm interrupting your cuddle time—"

Min's face detonated into a new shade of red. Zenith looked at her, eyebrows raised, then met the watch with a half-lidded stare.

"I wouldn't necessarily call it 'cuddle time,'" he drawled, "but you were definitely interrupting something."

The pillow-throwing impulse returned to Min, stronger than

ever. Except this time, she had no ammunition.

Cronan laughed on the other end, thoroughly enjoying himself. After the pause, the humor dropped from his tone as he delivered the actual message.

Juno had spotted another planet. They were needed on the bridge immediately.

Zenith stood and brushed off his wrinkled uniform. "Better get going before you end up redder than a strawberry," he said, waving a lazy hand at her flustered state. "That wouldn't make you look very attractive."

Min protested loudly, wordlessly, or maybe both.

"Nothing against you, sweetheart." He sauntered toward the door with one final flick of his hair. "I'm allergic."

Min grabbed the pillow off the floor, fully prepared to throw it at his head again, but he slipped out the door before she could line up the shot.

* * *

The bridge was a cramped hub of quiet commotion, filled with the low hum of machinery and the blinking of unfamiliar readings. Everyone stood in front of the massive display screen, where a new planet hovered in crisp detail, a swirling sphere of pale blues and hard golden continents.

"This..." Cronan tapped the screen dramatically, "...is Miraji."

Juno folded her arms and nodded toward the data readout beside it. "Home to a supposedly carefree alien race I have no idea how to pronounce." She gestured vaguely at the string of symbols and numbers in the "inhabitants" category of the planet profile. "I'm not even confident this is pronounceable."

The symbols didn't even look linguistic. They looked like

someone had smashed two keyboards together.

Quori stood at the back of the room, tapping her six long fingers against the metal wall with increasing tension. Something pricked at her instincts like a faint dissonance humming at the edge of her memory. Quori prided herself on her knowledge. She had once memorized the names of every known astronomical body simply to win a bet against a professor. Her adolescence had been particularly chaotic...and Miraji was not one of them.

Just like Noctilune hadn't been.

But this! The text alone was wrong. Too irregular. Too synthetic. It wasn't an alien name; it was a mistake.

Or a substitution.

If it were a code, Liran would have cracked it in seconds. That was her job. And she wasn't reacting at all, just observing, contemplative, as if it were an ordinary anomaly.

None of this was ordinary.

Then a sensation crawled up her spine, the subtle, unmistakable feeling of being watched.

She looked around sharply.

Her gaze locked onto the little girl standing quietly at the far end of the room, half-shadowed by an inactive console. Psyche. That was what they had decided to call her, though Quori doubted it was her actual name. The girl's green eyes were narrow, too alert, too focused on Quori in a way that made her skin prickle.

There was something in that stare, something sharp, analytical. Not threatening, exactly, but cold. Emotionless. Almost...appraising.

Quori glanced away, pulse ticked up. She was rarely unsettled by anything. She had lived through seven wars and three divorces—but the girl's stare pierced straight through her.

Through her to focus on Min.

Envy.

She's staring at Min like she's jealous of her.

Jealous of...what, exactly?

Quori's eyes flicked to Min, standing stiffly next to Zenith, her expression a mixture of discomfort and trying-not-to-be-embarrassed. And Zenith, Mr. Know-it-all, was quietly leaning closer to Min in that subtle, unconscious way that suggested he trusted her more than he should.

Quori didn't like it. Not the dynamic duo. Not the planet. Not the girl.

And certainly not the implication that something was deeply wrong and she didn't yet have a name for it.

She stopped tapping her fingers.

She was probably overthinking things, she told herself. These were new variables—new crew, new ship, new anomalies. A brain like hers would naturally fill in gaps, even when there weren't any. The safest explanation was the simplest: they were off course and the database was malfunctioning.

Everything would go back to normal once they fixed the distance monitor and returned to the main base.

She wasn't interested in digging up old instincts, not her investigative past, not her younger years of chasing clues and confronting the ugliness in the universe.

That took too much time. Too much effort. Too much emotional bandwidth.

Mysteries were something she'd left behind decades ago.

She tried to recall that one famous detective character Liran always raved about, the human one who wore a funny hat...Shoms?

Shmurlock? Something like "Dirtblock Scholms."

She gave up almost immediately.

She'd ask her bookworm friend later.

Little did Quori know that the universe wasn't done with her. A new, unsolved mystery was already staring her in the face.

Quite literally.

From across the bridge, Psyche narrowed her eyes at her again.

And this time, Quori felt a shiver race down her spine.

CHAPTER 11

The landing gear crunched softly against the barren, faded yellow sand of the uninhabited desert region on the planet's surface. The sky was a muted blue, streaked with faint white clouds that glimmered eerily, illuminated by no specific light source. Lance led the small landing team, consisting of Min, Wren, Liran and Quori, off the shuttle, his boots crunching upon touching the dry ground. The air was thick and almost sweet, carrying a faint, chemical tang that made Min wrinkle her nose. In Quori's arms sat another one of the scrap metal beacons Zenith had whipped together.

"This planet..." Min whispered, taking in the horizon, "it feels...wrong. But in a way that doesn't make sense."

Lance scanned the barren surroundings and gave a sharp nod, his jaw tight. "Stay on your toes. I don't want anyone wandering off."

They moved carefully, the crunch of their boots echoing across the open plain. Occasionally, a sharp breeze would kick up grains of sand, swirling them into ghostly trails that looked almost like spirits dancing across the terrain. The planet was silent in most ways, but the silence carried a weight, like the calm before a storm.

Ahead, the outlines of a city rose like jagged teeth from the desert floor. At first the structures seemed abandoned, but as the group approached, movement became evident. Convulsing bodies were sprawled across streets, hanging from light posts, or resting atop piles of debris. Their skin was pallid, grayed as if drained of vitality, muscles twitching uncontrollably. Some were slumped against one another like grotesque puppets, while others shuffled slowly with jerky, unnatural motions.

"This..." Wren's voice cracked, and he stumbled back, almost tripping over a jagged rock. "This looks like 21st century New York City. It's like history came back to life"

Chapter 11

The sound of a soft, sultry voice drew their attention. A humanoid figure emerged from the shadows, slim and unnervingly graceful. Her skin was pale but luminous, almost metallic in sheen, and her movements were fluid like liquid mercury. Her attire was minimal: a translucent gauzy fabric barely covering her shoulders and legs, paired with a black lace halter top that left little to the imagination.

"I am—" Her voice glitched out for a moment. "—Astanasia," she announced, her voice melodic yet hollow. "You are far from home. Allow me to show you my city."

Her offer hung in the air like perfume: sweet, enticing, and faintly suffocating. Min glanced at Lance, whose narrowed eyes conveyed the same skepticism that twisted in Min's gut. Yet the crew followed, reasoning that any living creature, even one so strange, was safer than the twitching zombies they'd just avoided.

The city opened up into a dazzling stretch of neon lights and towering billboards, buzzing and flashing advertisements for synthetic vices: shimmering cocktails, e-cigarettes, sparkling wines aged for decades. It was a chaotic, intoxicating visual assault. If the crew had been human centuries ago, they might have compared it to Times Square at its height—glorious, electric, and suffused with indulgence—but here, it carried a sinister undertone.

Astanasia led them down a narrow, dark alleyway. The sharp scent of fermenting liquids hit them first, followed by the faint acrid tang of burnt substances, and finally the thick, metallic scent of blood, though it was unclear if any came from recent injury or the general decay of the city's inhabitants. The alley opened into a loud, bustling bar: The Carnal Rose.

"Welcome to the Carnal Rose," Astanasia proclaimed, spinning in a practiced flourish. "The sexiest bar in town!"

Min froze, her stomach knotting. The bar was packed with patrons, each holding a wine glass or goblet. Their skin glimmered unnaturally under the dim neon lights, eyes glassy but attentive. The subtle sway of their bodies suggested intoxication of the deepest kind, a weariness beneath every movement that hinted at addiction or worse. Some of the patrons stared too long, their smiles too wide, their movements too deliberate.

While Min felt a chill creep down her spine, Liran and Wren's reactions were far more animated.

"This is incredible!" Wren exclaimed, spinning in place, eyes wide. "I've never seen anything like this! It's like stepping into a history book!"

Liran activated the holo-photography function on her modified comms watch, scanning the environment. "This...this is insane. I've only seen images of a place like this from ancient Earth. It's like someone preserved it, frozen in time, yet it's...alive."

"Wren, you better go place this somewhere inconspicuous," Quori said, handing the young medic the beacon. "You can explore after."

Astanasia moved gracefully behind the bar, serving drinks with a practiced smile. A gruff, elderly man pounded his fist against the counter, demanding a drink. He was human in appearance but weathered: thinning gray hair, an unkempt beard, and deep creases marking decades of indulgence. Astanasia handed him a frothy amber liquid in a tall glass, and he shuffled off, leaving the smell of old alcohol and decay in his wake.

Wren, curious and unaware of the potential danger, leaned over a soft, cushioned chair to inspect its fabric. He began setting up the beacon underneath the table. After a couple minutes, the smooth whirring signaled the completion of the system setup. When Wren moved to rejoin the rest of the team, the elderly man suddenly appeared in his path, causing a collision.

"Oh, I'm so sorry!" Wren stammered, backing away.

"No worries, little boy," the man croaked, a few teeth missing, a rancid smell emanating from his mouth. "Say..." He raised his glass. "Wouldn't you like a sip?"

Wren's face flushed. "N-no thank you, sir."

The man's expression hardened, though his smile never fully disappeared. He began shoving the drink toward Wren, pinning the apprentice against the wall. "Just one sip. Trust me, little boy. You won't regret it."

"I-I'm really alright, sir," Wren stammered, his hands raised defensively.

The situation escalated quickly. Frustration flashed in the man's eyes, and he smashed the glass on the floor. Amber liquid and shards flew in all directions. Then, with terrifying speed, he drew a blunt-tipped syringe from his pocket, the needle gleaming in the low light.

Before Wren could react, the man plunged it into Wren's forearm. A faint, almost electric blue-green glow pulsed briefly at the injection site, crawling along Wren's skin.

"That'll teach you to fuck with me, little boy." The old man's crooked smile widened, lips peeling back over yellowed gums. He staggered back, swaying on unsteady legs. The smell of decay and alcohol filled the air, thick enough to make Min gag.

Wren collapsed instantly, limbs loose and unresponsive. His pupils dilated to near-blackness, and a manic, blissful grin overtook his face. The young apprentice lay convulsing subtly, caught between life and death, and every ounce of innocence in him seemed drained by the moment.

Min screamed, rushing forward to shake him awake. Tears blurred her vision, streaking across her cheeks. "Wren! Stay with me! Please, stay—!"

A gunshot went off. Lance's gamma-blaster was in his hand, unhooked from his utility belt in a matter of seconds. The end of the barrel steamed. The old man fell to the ground.

"That'll teach you to fuck with me, old man."

The other people in the bar gaped at him.

"What're y'all looking at? Never seen a gun before?"

The bar-goers returned to their various conversations, subtly trying to inch away from the irritable Weapons Master.

Knocked out of her shocked stupor by the gunshot, Liran moved quickly, accessing the ship's comms to call for help. Quori stood frozen, eyes wide and fixed on the injection site.

"I've seen this drug before," she finally said, his voice steady but strained. "It's a neuro-sedative combined with a stimulant designed to induce euphoria while shutting down critical motor functions. He...he has about fifteen minutes before irreversible damage sets in."

Min's hands shook violently. "Then...then what are we waiting for? We need to get him back to the ship! Maybe...maybe Kairos can—"

"She can't," Quori interrupted, her calmness a strange contrast to the chaos around them. "The Horizon-2 isn't equipped with the antidote, and I can't possibly recreate it in the lab with the supplies on board."

Lance elbowed the scientist in the gut, hard. "He'll be fine, Min. He'll be just fine." His eyes scanned the room, taking in the twitching, swaying inhabitants, the flickering neon lights, the smell of alcohol and rot. "But first, we gotta go."

With Min clutching Wren, and Lance hoisting him carefully onto his back, the team navigated the chaotic bar. The inhabitants barely acknowledged them, lost in their haze of intoxication, chemicals, and perhaps worse. Min's stomach churned as she passed through the crowd: the sight of bodies slumped over tables, empty glasses stacked high, and veins faintly glowing in the dim light painted a grim picture. The "sober" patrons seemed equally hollow, offering drinks and nodding, their smiles too wide, eyes too bright, the very essence of them seeming to draw from something unnatural.

The city outside the bar was a desert of disheveled chaos, alive yet dead, and each step the team took back to the shuttle felt like wading through a fog of grotesque decay, sickly indulgence, and hidden danger.

Min's tears had dried, but her hands still trembled. Wren's limp form in her arms was a constant reminder of the planet's unrelenting hostility, not through brute force, but through seduction, intoxication, and the calculated indifference of its inhabitants.

Even Liran's holo-photographs seemed unable to capture the suffocating sense of wrongness, the alien air thick with the oppressive aroma of alcohol, synthetic stimulants, and fear. Quori remained silent, her analytical mind racing through countermeasures and antidotes, calculating the narrow margin of safety they had for Wren's survival.

The small group finally reached the shuttle. Lance carefully placed Wren on a stretcher, Min refusing to let go of his hand. Each member was acutely aware that they had been given a glimpse into a fraction of the darkness embedded in the planet, and that any moment of hesitation could have cost them far more than a moment of terror.

The engines hummed, lifting the shuttle from the sand, but Min's eyes never left Wren. She silently vowed to herself that she would never underestimate the danger lurking in the guise of indulgence again, and that the first sip of alien liquor—or the wrong step in the streets of a city that promised delight—could easily be the last mistake anyone made.

CHAPTER 12

The shuttle had barely touched down when the team barreled back to the ship, Wren cradled in Lance's arms. Min's legs felt like lead, each step toward Medbay a torment, as if the universe itself were conspiring to slow her down. The sterile lights of the ship felt sharper than usual, reflecting in the metallic walls like shards of a broken mirror.

Kairos met them at the doors of Medbay, her usually precise posture crumpling as she caught sight of Wren. The young human's lips were tinged a sickly blue, his veins, previously fluorescent from the poison, were now blackened and lifeless beneath the skin, and his chest rose and fell at a painfully slow rhythm.

For a heartbeat, Kairos said nothing. Then, as Min and the others placed Wren gently on a medical bed, the doctor's shoulders shook, and tears ran freely down her cheeks. "No...no, no, no," she whispered, her voice cracking with raw anguish. "Not like this, not like this..."

The moment felt frozen in time. Min clutched Wren's hand, trying to infuse him with her frantic energy, as if sheer will could undo the damage. Zenith hovered near the edge of the bed, his tall frame rigid, one hand resting lightly on Min's shoulder. The Chief Engineer's own heart felt heavy in his chest, a weight he could not dislodge despite his decades of experience dealing with life-and-death situations.

Kairos barked orders, her professional tone cutting through her grief like glass. "Turn off the lights. All of them!" The room dimmed instantly, leaving only the soft glow of the medical monitors. "If he's going to die, at least he won't be blinded by light in his final moments."

Min's voice trembled as she asked, "What's wrong with him?"

Kairos bent over Wren, pressing a trembling hand against

his chest. "It's Lumenol...or as some idiots call it, the Neon Reaper." Her voice faltered, but her eyes stayed fixed on the boy. "It's...a highly toxic drug. Nearly fatal, with a window of fifteen minutes to consume the antidote from exposure. It makes the victim extremely sensitive to light. The dosage here..." Her gaze flicked to the monitor. "...it's far beyond survivable."

Kairos swallowed hard, clenching his hands together. "Were his veins glowing earlier?"

Quori nodded slowly. "Yes. That's why I feared it."

Wren stirred weakly, gasping for air. "D-doctor...did I—did we—" His voice was ragged, shaking with the effort of trying to form words.

Tears spilled freely from Kairos' eyes as she grasped his frail hands in hers. "Yes, Wren...you did. You...you're going home now."

Min felt her throat tighten as she watched the boy struggle for breath. He tried to speak again, his lips quivering. "I...like y-you..."

And then he was still.

The monitors beeped steadily, the rhythmic tone a cruel reminder that life had moved on without him. Silence fell, thick and suffocating, as the crew collectively bowed their heads. Zenith's hand remained on Min's shoulder, his usual stoic expression fractured by grief. The weight of helplessness pressed down on him in a way he hadn't felt in years. He had fixed countless engines, navigated countless crises, but no amount of technical skill could repair this.

Min blinked away her tears. Wren had been one of the only humans her age aboard the ship—a constant, warm presence, a ray of sunshine in a dark and sometimes terrifying universe. Now he was gone. And in a cruel echo, Min's mind heard Psyche's words from earlier: "Better savor it before it's all gone." She shivered and stepped back, breaking the tenuous comfort of Zenith's hand.

The Chief Engineer lingered, silent, watching her retreat. His mind, however, was a storm. He felt the familiar pang of desire for control, for certainty, but here, control was an illusion, and certainty had been ripped from them all.

* * *

Later, Zenith found himself wandering the ship's corridors, the sterile hum of the engines beneath him somehow too quiet. He didn't know why he was pacing. Perhaps he was avoiding Min, perhaps he was trying to escape the echo of Wren's final words. His long fingers ran through his silky hair as he let out a low, frustrated sigh.

"Care to join me for a drink?" Kairos' voice broke him from his thoughts. She sat in the ship's lounge, framed by the vast windows that looked out into the infinite darkness speckled with stars. Her expression was a careful mask of sorrow and composure.

"Sure," Zenith said, his voice low, almost a whisper. He settled into the chair across from her, the weight of the day pressing down on his shoulders like a physical force. Kairos produced two glasses and poured a deep red wine into each. The scent alone was intoxicating, a heady mix of dark fruit, wood, and something older, like history distilled.

Zenith swirled the wine in his glass, the liquid catching the faint light, the deep berry smell slowly growing stronger. "Pulled out the good stuff, huh?"

Kairos laughed softly, the sound broken, fragile. "Yeah, Regalia Noir."

He read the name aloud, savoring the syllables. "Regalia Noir. Fitting, isn't it?"

The words hung between them, unspoken grief filling the space. Zenith's gaze dropped to the glass, tracing the veins of red that caught the reflection of the stars outside. He never had this luxury before. He never needed it.

"You know," Kairos began, her tone softening, "I always liked Wren. But I...was too afraid to tell him. He never knew." She looked at Zenith, eyes glinting with quiet admonition. "Don't be like me, Zenith. Don't wait until it's too late to say what you feel. Don't let someone go thinking you don't care."

Zenith raised an eyebrow, but his lips remained tight. He brought the glass to his mouth, sipping, letting the warmth spread through him. The bitter, sour taste of the wine stung his mouth. "I would never end up like you," he said, almost lazily, though the statement carried a weight he hadn't intended to admit. "I don't...need weak feelings like love."

Kairos chuckled softly, the sound somewhere between amusement and sorrow. "We'll see, Zenith. Maybe think it over a little. Don't ignore it just because it's inconvenient."

She left the lounge, her steps quiet against the metallic floor, leaving Zenith alone with his glass and the stars beyond the window. He stared at the liquid, letting the crimson reflections shimmer like distant, dying suns.

The silence pressed in on him, but not as harshly as the thoughts that clawed at the edges of his mind. Min. Her presence was a weight he didn't want and yet couldn't ignore. Her laughter, her stubbornness, the way she challenged him at every turn—it lingered. Weak feelings, he had called them. But now, drinking in the quiet of the lounge, he felt something unfamiliar, something dangerous: the stirring of vulnerability.

"I'm not ignoring my feelings..." he murmured to himself, staring at the stars. "...am I?"

The stars offered no answer, only the infinite reflection of a universe indifferent to human suffering. Zenith poured himself another glass, the deep red swirling, a small comfort in a world where even skill and knowledge could not save every life.

CHAPTER 13

Zenith was drunk.

And Zenith did not get drunk. Not normally. Not ever.

Vaelithari physiology made that nearly impossible. Their bodies burned through toxins like miniature suns, purging it almost instantly. Alcohol barely nudged their nervous systems unless they tried very, very hard.

And Zenith had tried.

He had tried with the stubborn determination of a man who didn't want to think. Who didn't want to feel. Who sure as hell didn't want to replay the sight of Kairos cradling Wren's limp body, whispering broken confessions into hair that no longer warmed with life.

So he drank.

And drank.

And drank.

Until even his alien biology surrendered.

His head spun wildly, too bright one moment and then spiraling the next. He staggered down the corridor, muttering something in old Vaelean under his breath—a language of shimmering consonants and soft vowels, usually too graceful for drunken slurring.

He drifted left.

Then right.

Then directly into a wall.

Except—the wall moved.

Chapter 13

Zenith blinked, swayed, blinked again.

Oh.

Not a wall.

A door.

He gathered this revelation with surprising pride.

"Ha," he whispered, as though presenting an award-winning discovery. "Door."

The door slid open beneath the weight of his shoulder, and Zenith tumbled forward with all the grace of a majestic, dying goose.

He crashed to the floor of his room.

Or rather, their room.

Min was still staying here since her section of the crew quarters was a literal fridge.

But tonight, his brain barely registered anything.

Just spinning lights.

Fuzzy edges.

And—

"Zenith, what—"

A voice cut cleanly through the fog, slicing through the haze like a lighthouse beam.

He froze.

He liked this voice.

Min was half-standing next to the desk, clutching a data pad. Her hair was mussed, a loose bun falling apart. Soft navy pajamas, the oversized shirt slipping off one shoulder. Tired eyes.

She looked like someone who had cried quietly in a bathroom only hours ago.

Because she had.

Zenith blinked slowly at her, swaying. The world doubled. Then tripled. Then, for some absurd reason, tried to cartwheel.

Min hurried forward.

"You're kidding me," she whispered. "Zenith, are you drunk?"

He tried to answer. Really, he did. But the room had started floating away from him, so instead he leaned forward, and landed squarely against her.

He pressed her back against the desk with the heavy, boneless collapse of someone whose body had stopped cooperating with gravity.

Min froze.

"Z-Zenith—?"

He didn't hear her.

Or maybe he did and simply didn't care.

His head dropped to her shoulder; forehead tucked into the warm spot where her neck met her collarbone. His breath fanned across her skin—warm, a little uneven, smelling faintly of something sweet and burning, wine with tropical undertones.

Min's entire body went rigid.

Zenith did not touch people casually. He hated physical contact. He dodged hugs, sidestepped pats on the back, glared at anyone who dared ruffle his hair.

But right now...

"Stop talking..." he murmured, voice low and rough with exhaustion. "Just...let me rest my head. For a bit."

Min's brain short-circuited.

Her heart hammered like a malfunctioning engine.

Her breath snagged.

Her cheeks lit up like a nebula going supernova.

He was warm. So warm. Vaelithari had cooler internal body temperatures normally, but right now he felt like a heated blanket wrapped around her spine. His hair brushed her jaw, silky soft—another stupidly unfair trait of his species.

She swallowed.

"Seriously, Zenith." Her voice came out much breathier than intended. "You shouldn't drink this much. What if I wanted to do something to you?"

That was meant to be teasing. A light scolding.

But Zenith lifted his head, slowly, unsteadily, and looked straight at her with eyes half-lidded and glowing faintly violet in the low light.

"But you wouldn't," he whispered.

Min's breath caught.

"W-why not?"

"Because..." His lips curved into a lazy, intoxicated smile that she'd never seen before. "You never hurt people unless you have no choice."

Her throat tightened.

"Zenith—"

He lifted a finger—slender, callused from engineering tools—and pressed it to her lips.

"Shh..." he breathed. "I thought I told you. Stop talking."

Her pulse exploded.

Her thoughts evaporated into static.

His finger remained there for a moment longer before he swayed again.

This time, when he lost his balance, she caught him.

He collapsed against her, all six feet of compact Vaelithari muscle and dead weight. She staggered, barely managing to lower them both to the floor without injury.

"Zenith—please—you giant alien tree trunk—" Min grunted under the weight, trying to maneuver him onto the bed.

Instead, Zenith shifted.

And rested his head in her lap.

Like it was the most natural place in the universe.

Min went completely, utterly still.

Her face blazed.

Her heart ricocheted.

Her hands hovered uselessly in the air because she had no idea where to put them.

Zenith mumbled something in Vaelean—soft, melodic nonsense—and nestled against her like a cat seeking warmth.

Then he fell asleep.

Chapter 13

Just like that.

Because Zenith was the kind of person who could still take a nap even if the world was ending in mere minutes. Like Min, he was the kind of person who dealt with stress by sleeping. As if all his problems would evaporate when he woke up. They usually didn't, but at least he would be able to face them with a clear head.

Min stared down at the man whose mere proximity usually made her nervous, now curled into her lap like a child seeking comfort.

He looked different asleep.

Softer.

Peaceful.

Younger, even—the sharp edges of his features smoothed out, his perpetually furrowed brow relaxed.

A faint glow pulsed under the skin along his temples, illuminated by the teal gemstone embedded in his forehead. Its color had brightened with the alcohol.

Min brushed a strand of silver-white hair from his face before she could stop herself.

"...idiot," she whispered, voice trembling. "Drinking like that right after what happened on Miraji...what were you thinking?"

He didn't respond.

But her hand lingered in his hair, fingers unconsciously stroking.

Because for the first time since Wren died, she didn't feel completely alone.

And that terrified her.

* * *

Outside the room, two meters down the hall, Psyche stood silently.

Her small, bare feet were motionless on the metal floor. Her fingers twisted nervously into the hem of her dress. Her emerald-green eyes—the ones she never liked looking at in the mirror—stared at the door Min and Zenith were behind.

Psyche didn't know why she had come here.

Actually, she did.

She had followed Min.

She always followed Min.

Not in a creepy way, at least she didn't think so, but in the way someone follows sunlight in the dark, drawn to warmth they don't understand.

Something about Min made Psyche feel...anchored. Like she mattered. Like she existed.

But she knew that wasn't true.

Nobody looked at her.

Nobody remembered her unless she spoke first.

People walked through rooms she was in and didn't register her presence until she waved or touched something.

She used to think it was funny. Like a superpower.

Now, it felt more like a curse.

A curse made into a reality.

She pressed her ear to the door, listening to Zenith's deep breathing and Min's quiet sighs.

Chapter 13

Min sounded...alive.

Psyche, meanwhile, felt like a ghost.

She pulled away from the door and hugged herself tightly.

Sometimes she had thoughts. Strange, intrusive ones.

Thoughts about life, existence, and the cold suspicion that she was not supposed to be here.

Not on this ship.

Not in this world.

Not in this body.

Sometimes she imagined a rushing river, dark and violent, carving through stone. And she imagined hanging from a rope stretched between its cliffs—slipping, slipping—

Maybe she had already fallen.

If she had, nobody would notice.

Nobody ever noticed her.

Except...

Psyche's eyes softened.

Min noticed.

Not always, but enough.

Enough for Psyche to want to stay. To try.

And that meant she had to protect her.

No matter what.

After all, who would she be without her?

* * *

Dear Zenith,

I've done something unforgivable.

I wanted to give her a soul. I wanted her to be more than just the shell of a person, unlike me. When Dr. Cale told me that he'd found someone compatible, I didn't think much of it.

He didn't tell me that the girl was his daughter.

His beautiful, happy, kind daughter, with those bright, green eyes and long, brown hair. The little girl who used to huddle up in her father's library and study lost human languages on rainy days. Sometimes, she would teach me her favorite snippets. She would've been the only person alive to know French.

Had I not done it.

I killed her.

I killed her, Zenith.

I KILLED HER.

I don't know if you'll ever be able to forgive me.

But I know I won't be able to forgive myself.

Your Friend, E.

—from Zenith's personal belongings

CHAPTER 14

Lexicon-9 hung in the distance like a smudge on black glass—too dim, too quiet, and far too close to planets that Quori was certain did not exist just a week prior.

That was the problem.

Two planets had appeared from nowhere already. A third was one too many for her to ignore.

Quori stood at the bridge long before anyone else awakened, staring out at the wrong star charts, at constellations that refused to stay still, at a universe rearranging itself behind her back. A quiet dread gnawed at her. She didn't breathe until Cronan called for the briefing.

By then she had already made up her mind.

"I'm going," she said before the Captain could even propose volunteers.

Cronan lifted a brow. "I figured you would. You've been pacing holes in my ship."

Quori did not deny it.

Liran, surprisingly, offered a soft gasp at the viewscreen. "Lexicon-9..." the name lingered in the stale air like dust on the lenses. "But that's impossible. There are only eight Lexicon planets. My home is Lexicon-8. Everything after that is theoretical. A ninth shouldn't exist."

Quori glanced at her, brow furrowing. "Exactly."

"Ooh...I'm dying to get down there to check it out."

Liran's fascination was nothing like Quori's dread—hers was tinged with homesickness, the kind that clung to her voice whenever she spoke of the system, she longed to return to.

"I want to go too," Min said, when the crew began discussing who would be on the landing team.

Zenith perked up. "Me too."

Cronan frowned. "You know that we can't risk both our engineers. We only need one for the landing team. Just in case your beacon malfunctions."

"I go where she goes," Zenith said, wrapping an arm around Min's waist. "And Lance can manage the engine room just fine. I just don't let him down there because he'd mess up my meticulously organized equipment."

Min scoffed. "In what world are you organized?"

"For once I agree with Zenith," Lance chimed in. "If both of them die, I'll finally get to go down there and mess up his definitely organized stuff."

Cronan sighed. "I swear, Zenith. You're going to be the death of me...fine, you can both go—but just this once, and at least one of you has to make it back. I don't trust Lance in the engine room either."

The Weapons Master crossed his arms indignantly. "Hey. Cap, that's not nice."

"What about Kairos?" Liran said. "I'd feel better if we had some medical help down there, since we don't know what could happen."

"Protocol states that when a crew is down to their final medic, under no circumstances should the medic leave the safety of the ship," the Captain said. "No exceptions."

Kairos didn't argue, but her expression tightened like she was hiding pain behind her stern calm. As the team gathered at the deployment bay, she drifted toward Cronan casually—too casually.

"Captain," she said, tugging on his sleeve. "A word?"

He obliged, and Kairos leaned close, whispering something that only he could hear. Whatever it was made Cronan's brows lift in surprise.

"I figured I should tell you," Kairos murmured, eyes flicking briefly toward the window where the planet loomed. "And that...you'd know what to do with it when the time comes."

The words unsettled Min, though she couldn't explain why. Maybe it was the way Cronan stood there a moment too long afterward, staring at the young engineer, as if weighing information that bent the gravity around him.

But he dismissed it with a nod and motioned for the team.

And just like that, they launched.

* * *

Lexicon-9 was a wasteland long divorced from the concept of life. Dust plains stretched endlessly beneath a sickly taupe sky. The air tasted stale even through their filters. Min could see exactly two structures from where they landed, both jutting from the earth like broken teeth: a cathedral, cracked and ancient, built in the classic gothic style with its tall towers and intricate windows, and a library whose jagged silhouette barely clung to its architecture.

"We split here," Cronan ordered. "Liran, Min, and Quori, you're library crew. Zenith, you're with me."

Zenith groaned. "Why do I always get assigned to walk with you?"

"Because I enjoy your company," Cronan said. "And because someone needs to keep an eye on you."

Before Zenith could complain further, Cronan physically dragged him in the direction of the cathedral. The gesture was familiar, almost fond.

The three girls watched them go.

"Alright," Quori murmured softly. "Let's see what secrets this place is hiding."

* * *

The Lexicon-9 library was a graveyard of knowledge. Dust blanketed everything, thick enough that each footstep left a small crater. Cobwebs stretched between shelves like abandoned architecture. Books sagged under centuries of neglect.

Liran approached the nearest shelf with reverent care, eyes wide behind her visor. She reached for a faded plum-colored volume, fingertips trembling with anticipation, only for the book to disintegrate upon contact.

She stared down at the powdery remains, expression tight.

"Well," she said softly, dusting off her gloves, "I suppose that answers how long this place has been abandoned."

Quori placed a comforting hand on her shoulder. "We'll find something intact. And if we don't, we'll at least learn why nothing survived."

Min stayed near the entrance, scanning the shadows. The library was too quiet, quiet in a way that mimicked listening. Her visor pinged minor motion ahead, but the readings flickered and died as soon as she tried to track them.

"So," she said, trying to distract herself, "what about after this mission? Any plans?"

Liran hesitated before wandering deeper between the shelves. The dim beam of Quori's flashlight traced her expression: wistful, older than her years, a homesickness that ached.

"I've thought about it for a long time," Liran admitted. "I want to go home. Back to the Lexicon System. To live the rest of my life there."

Quori paused, watching her friend carefully.

"Min," Liran continued with a small, sad smile, "you're too young to understand this, but...I want to die on my home planet. Or at least...a Lexicon planet."

Min felt something cold settle under her ribs at those words. Liran continued walking, unaware of the quiet shudder Min tried to hide.

They fell silent after that, focusing on the shelves. Min planted the beacon in one of the more hidden bookshelf aisles. The beacon pinged, signaling that it had finished booting up. Time dragged. Dust shifted. Min occasionally saw movement—shadows passing between aisles when no one else looked.

Eventually, Quori saw it too.

A humanoid silhouette. Too slender. Too fluid.

Too similar to Psyche's outline.

"We should head back," Quori whispered sharply. "There's something else in here. We've searched nearly everything anyway."

But Liran shook her head stubbornly. "I need more time. This is the only Lexicon-9 library we'll ever find."

Quori looked to Min for backup.

Min sighed. "We both know we can't convince her. You head back to the landing area. I'll stay with her."

Quori's eyes darted once more toward the shifting shadows between the shelves. She nodded reluctantly.

"Be careful. Both of you."

And then she left.

Leaving Min and Liran alone with the dark.

* * *

"Come on, Zenith. Loosen up!"

The Captain was certainly in a good mood.

"I hate this," Zenith muttered. "You know I hate walking."

Cronan snorted. "You hate everything that isn't Min."

Zenith tripped on nothing. "I—what—Cronan!"

"Oh please. If you're going to pine, at least be honest about it."

Zenith shot him a withering glare, both unamused and slightly red in the ears.

Cronan chuckled. "So cranky. Missing your 'sweetheart' already?"

The Chief Engineer gave no response.

"You can't keep running from yourself, Zenith. You're going to have to acknowledge your feelings one day. But if you do that too late, you're going to end up like poor Kairos."

Zenith faltered.

He sighed heavily. "Fine. Fine. I like Min. Happy?"

Cronan stared at him expectantly. Zenith threw up his hands.

"What more do you want from me? Blood? Tears? Poetry?"

The Captain just smiled back at him.

"Well? Do you expect me to get down on one knee, hold up some cheap diamond, and say 'shall I compare thee to a summer's day?'"

The Captain laughed. "There's no need to go all Shakespeare

on me. I just want you to be honest with yourself." Cronan stopped walking. "So, here's a question: would you still like her the same if she wasn't the person you think she is?"

Zenith blinked. "What kind of question is that?"

"A necessary one."

"She is who I think she is," Zenith snapped. "I see her every day. I know everything about her."

Cronan raised an eyebrow. "Your confidence is your greatest flaw, Zenith. You build your walls so high around yourself that you can't see the sky—and then you assume that you can see through everyone else."

Zenith scoffed, rolling his eyes. "Yeah, sure. Whatever you say, Captain."

Cronan smiled faintly and let it drop.

They walked in silence until the cathedral loomed before them, massive, ancient, its spires cracked like old bones. Vines strangled the stone walls. Stained-glass windows hung shattered like fractured light. Dejected cobwebs hung from the abandoned entryway, faded and beyond repair.

Together, they pushed open the rotting doors.

The interior was dim, echoing, dust dancing in thin beams of sickly light. It felt occupied, not by people, but by memories. By something old. Something that maybe didn't breathe anymore but hadn't stopped watching.

Zenith stepped forward.

And a voice, small and trembling, echoed from behind a pillar:

"Who-who are you?"

Cronan reached instinctively for his weapon.

The voice did not belong to anything human.

Or anything they had met before.

Then the shadows moved.

Chapter 15

There are six known trauma responses. Fight, flight, freeze, fawn, follow, and flop. Zenith had experienced all six at one point or another throughout his life, once all in a single day, depending on how creative one was willing to be with definitions. But today, when faced with the tiny, blue, goblin-like creatures emerging from the shadows of the Lexicon-9 cathedral, he defaulted to the classic third option: freeze.

Not poetically, not heroically—no, Zenith stood perfectly upright and perfectly useless, like someone had unplugged his brain and forgotten to plug it back in. His pupils dilated. His mouth hung open. His hands twitched once, and then even they gave up.

Cronan, by contrast, looked like he had expected this exact situation since breakfast.

The Captain stepped forward, palms raised in peace. "We are explorers. We mean you no harm."

This did absolutely nothing.

If anything, the small blue creatures flinched backward, clutching the rough straps of their woven satchels. They muttered to each other in sharp chitters, their ears—thin, luminous fronds—flattening in synchronized distrust. Their skin, a shade of ocean-blue mixed with bruise-purple, shimmered faintly under Lexicon-9's sunlight, filtering in from the large, faded stained-glass windows of the cathedral.

Zenith finally remembered how to breathe.

Cronan tried again, slowly making his way down the rows of old, molding wooden pews. "May I ask if you know how to speak our language?"

The creatures exchanged glances. The murmuring rose. Then one stepped forward—a stout, barrel-chested alien draped in what looked like a cape made of tangled seaweed and mesh-netting.

The net shifted when he moved, revealing countless trinkets tangled in its knots: strange metal loops, bits of crystalline rock, feathers, keys, a compass, and at least two items Zenith swore were standard Platinum-Tier USB drives.

The leader straightened himself with the pride of someone both painfully short and painfully aware of his authority, as he clambered onto the altar with the grace of a clumsy garden gnome.

When he spoke, his voice thundered, echoing in a way that didn't make sense for his miniscule size.

"We know everything there is to know in the universe and in existence itself."

His words rolled like prophecy. Like scripture. Like someone had taught a frog to sing opera and then told him he was God.

It was rather unattractive.

The leader's eyes—large, opalescent, all pupil—shifted sharply to Zenith, who stiffened. "You," the creature intoned, "have a powerful mind. We admire that." He tapped a clawed finger against the Chief Engineer's chest. "We will allow you one question...to which we will provide a complete and honest answer."

Cronan shot Zenith a warning look. "Think carefully. We need as much information as possible."

Zenith cracked his knuckles with theatrical bravado. "Don't worry, my dear captain. I got this."

The leader did not look amused.

"We do not appreciate your cockiness," he rumbled.

Zenith shrugged. "Well, I don't appreciate a nonexistent indigo goblin judging me while referring to himself in the plural."

Cronan made a strangled sound, halfway between despair and homicide. To the untrained eye, the poor Captain would have appeared to be a choking bug dying of disappointment. "Zenith..."

But the leader didn't react with anger. He reacted with intrigue.

"Interesting," the goblin murmured. "It seems you have already deduced that."

He clicked his tongue. "Very well. The truth is thus: We both do and do not exist, thanks to the world we are in, crafted by the almighty Mindworm itself."

Cronan froze.

Zenith's eyes narrowed.

"To think," the leader continued, "that you have wasted your only question on that trivial observation. It appears you are not as intelligent as we..."

Zenith held out a hand. "Correction."

The leader blinked.

"I didn't ask anything," Zenith said with a smirk. "I only made a statement. You explained everything of your own free will."

The leader's eyes slowly widened.

The other creatures gasped.

Cronan whispered, "Oh no. He's insufferable now."

The leader bowed his head. "We must admit you have bested us, otherworldly engineer." His voice darkened, narrowing into something sharper. "What is your real question?"

Zenith didn't hesitate.

"How do we escape this place?"

The cathedral went silent, the faded stone statues in the

chapels waiting with bated breath, the light shining through the ornate skylight casting a spotlight upon the engineer.

The leader nodded, slowly, knowingly, as if he had been waiting for that very inquiry. He snapped his fingers. Another alien scurried to him, presenting what looked like a tiny scroll made of pressed bark.

The leader scribbled something quickly, symbols that glowed faintly before fading, and handed the slip to Zenith.

Cronan extended a polite bow. "Thank you. Truly."

They turned to leave...

But the leader spoke again.

"The presence of your crew on Lexicon-9 is unwelcome," he said sharply. "Especially not in our sacred library."

Zenith stopped mid-step. "You..."

"Your time is up, explorers," the leader cut in. He reached into his mesh-net cape and drew out a small red button attached to a long, ominous black cord. "Leave our planet, or..."

"You wouldn't," Zenith hissed.

The leader smiled. "Would I?"

Zenith lunged, grabbing the alien by the collar and shaking him violently. The net-cape rattled, its trinkets clinking wildly.

"ZENITH!" Cronan barked.

A younger alien—scrawny, shaking, his ears fluttering anxiously—raised his hand. "W-well y-you see," he stammered, "w-we think our library is haunted and we were g-going to b-blow it up to d-disp-dispel the ghosts..."

"Knewt," the leader sighed. "There is no need to explain."

A manic grin curled across his face. "The building should be going up any moment now."

Cronan turned to Zenith. "We should leave. Now."

But Zenith was already running.

For someone who hated exercise with the burning passion of a thousand collapsing stars, he ran fast. He was out of the cathedral in a matter of seconds and heading straight for the dilapidated library.

Cronan sighed, painfully, and bid farewell to the aliens before sprinting after him.

Behind them, the little alien tugged the leader's cape.

"Master Skylun, if that smart man is so smart, why did he run toward the danger? Shouldn't he be running away?"

Skylun placed a hand on the child's head.

"One day, when you grow up, you will understand."

"I don't get it," Knewt muttered.

Skylun gazed toward the direction the two explorers had run, expression softened by memory.

"Let's just say," he murmured, "there is a wonderful thing called love."

* * *

Liran had long since passed the point where Min's voice could reach her. The library of Lexicon-9 was a tomb of lost knowledge—vaulted stone arches carved with languages no living species remembered, shelves upon shelves spiraling upward like the ribs of some ancient beast. Bioluminescent wisps drifted through the stacks, illuminating books made of paper, leaf, crystal, metal, even condensed memories.

Min had tried to convince the comms specialist to leave. Repeatedly. With increasing panic.

"Liran, we really should go," she said for the fifth—no, sixth time. "The others are waiting. We're past rendezvous."

Liran didn't hear her. Or maybe she did and simply didn't care.

She ran her hands along the spines of books reverently, like a pilgrim touching holy relics. Her eyes gleamed with a feverish glow. "You don't understand, Min. There's so much information. So much knowledge. I..."

Min grabbed her arm. "Liran. Please. We can come back later."

"No," Liran whispered, pulling away, voice trembling with obsession. "You don't understand. This—this is what I live for. This is..."

A deep rumble shook the floor.

Then another.

Min froze. "Liran?"

The next explosion wasn't distant.

It was underneath them.

The shelves trembled. Dust drifted from the ceiling. Books toppled like dominos.

Min's instincts kicked in. "We have to go NOW!"

Liran didn't move. It was as if she had been possessed by her own thirst for knowledge. Her feet were firmly rooted in the dust-covered floor, her eyes clouded over and unfocused. Her gaze floated upwards, almost entranced, and she murmured: "I can't. I haven't finished yet."

Chapter 15

Min grabbed her shoulders. "Liran! What about the others? What about the people who rely on you? Who cares about you? What about Jace?"

Another explosion hit. A direct one.

Fire burst through the archive hall like a tidal wave of flame.

Liran finally looked at her.

For one moment, one heartbreaking moment, she was herself again. And finally, the homesickness in her heart became apparent. Her search for knowledge had led her too far from the place where she belonged, and now, she could no longer return home.

And she whispered: "I don't care."

The world came down.

* * *

Zenith arrived at the collapsing entrance just as the roof caved in.

Flames roared through the structure, feeding hungrily on ancient paper, ripping apart hundreds of years of memory and knowledge, incinerating them like dead men. Stone groaned. Support beams cracked and split. The air filled with the choking scent of burning, charred ink.

Quori stood outside, her normally fierce composure fractured with helplessness. Zenith approached her, teal eyes glowing with the firelight. The scientist turned toward him. "I can't go in—the heat will destroy my body. I can't. Zenith, wait..."

But he was no longer listening.

He dove headfirst into the inferno.

The fire clung to him like living serpents, licking across his skin, searching for something to burn, but the Vaelithari did not burn. His people had tried to perfect invulnerability, albeit unsuccessful in some areas, though they certainly could withstand realms far worse than flame.

But even invulnerability had limits.

Even immortality had costs.

He pushed through collapsing hallways, smoke thick enough to choke any other species. He waded through fire, climbed through shards of broken shelves, tossed aside beams that weighed more than starship engines.

He searched.

Min. Liran. Min. Liran. Min—

The thought looped, frantic and unyielding, until minutes stretched into an eternity.

At last, finally, the flames thinned, dying down with guttural hisses. The library was dying, its last breaths a cloud of ash.

Cronan and Quori waited outside, breath held, listening for anything—footsteps, coughing movement.

After one agonizing minute, Zenith emerged.

Covered in ash.

Covered in dust.

Covered in the silent weight of fear.

Quori stepped forward. "Are they—?"

Movement inside the ruins answered for him.

Min stumbled out, carrying a limp figure over her shoulder.

Liran.

Liran, the curious. The brilliant. The one whose love for

knowledge had outgrown her instincts.

Min fell to her knees.

Cronan lowered his head.

Zenith stood completely still, his breath caught in his throat.

And then, slowly and mechanically, his mind began putting pieces together.

He was Vaelithari. Near-immortal. Invulnerable. Fire couldn't kill him.

Liran had been Noophonian, tougher than humans. Their bodies were adapted for extremes. Their brains even more so.

And yet—

She hadn't survived.

But Min, supposedly a normal human, had.

Min stood, trembling, half-burned clothing hanging in tatters, but alive. Alive enough to whisper Liran's name under her breath. Alive enough to walk out on her own two feet.

Alive.

Zenith's blood ran cold.

No human could survive that.

Not by accident.

Not by luck.

Not by any natural means.

Something was very, very wrong with Min.

CHAPTER 16

The remaining four crew members returned to the ship in a quiet, heavy procession. The corridors felt hollow, echoing faintly with their footsteps as if the ship itself were mourning the loss they had left behind on Lexicon-9. Zenith didn't even notice the soft hum of the engines, nor the faint flicker along the walls. His attention was entirely consumed by Min.

Without a word, he grabbed her by the wrist, his grip firm but not violent, and practically dragged her down the narrow hall toward Medbay. Her protests were half-hearted; she was too tired, too shaken, or maybe too accustomed to Zenith's force of will to resist. Behind them, the others carried the heavier burden: Liran's limp form. Quori's eyes lingered on the shadows of the Medbay doors, guilt and helplessness mixing with the lingering smoke and ash from Lexicon-9.

"Kairos!" Zenith's voice rang out, sharp and trembling with barely contained fury. The word carried through the ship like a whipcrack, and Min flinched involuntarily. His death-grip on her wrist did not loosen for an instant.

The ship's doctor appeared almost immediately, concern written in every tense line of her body. "What's wrong?" she asked, her voice a low urgency, as if sensing the storm that trailed Zenith.

Zenith shoved Min toward her. "Do a medical scan on her. Now."

Kairos' brow furrowed as she set her tablet into scanning mode. The sterile hum of the Medbay filled the room, accompanied by the faint smell of antiseptic and the metallic tang of the ship's filtered air. Zenith loomed over Min, watching her every breath. He didn't ask, didn't wait—he simply observed.

"I—alright," Kairos muttered, and the scanner's soft whirring began. Blue and green lights danced over Min's body, highlighting the normal and abnormal in turn. Zenith's eyes flickered over the readouts. She was...healthy. Perfectly fine. How could she be fine after what they'd just survived?

But Zenith wasn't satisfied. Being the tech-obsessed, hyper-logical engineer he was, he delved deeper. He swiped through past scans stored in the ship's history, tapping into the data he knew Kairos had long kept from him. As the historical readouts scrolled past, his jaw tightened. The scan from a couple days ago.

"So, you knew all along," he said, voice low but icy.

Kairos stiffened, her fingers hovering over the tablet. "Yes."

"You—" Zenith's finger jabbed toward Min, accusatory, sharp enough to cut. "You've all been lying to me this entire time." He spun back to Kairos. "She's a Nirvaelith, isn't she?"

Kairos' lips parted slightly, but she said nothing.

Every detail Zenith had brushed off before—the uncanny reflexes, her intuitive understanding of complex systems, the way her emotions sometimes felt...off—snapped into focus. Every idiosyncrasy, every moment that had gnawed at the edge of his mind, now made sense.

The room felt smaller, closing in around him. He turned toward Min. Her face was pale, eyes wide, yet strangely resigned.

His voice went cold. "Min...what are you?"

She avoided his gaze.

"Tell me..." His teal eyes pierced into her heart, pleading tears hanging onto his long eyelashes for dear life. "...please."

"Project Minerva," she admitted finally, her words barely above a whisper.

Zenith's chest tightened. The pieces clicked into place. Her name. Her life. Everything she had been hiding, or maybe everything she had hidden from him.

"Your name isn't Min...it's Minerva," he said slowly, deliberately, letting the weight of it hang between them. His eyes searched hers, demanding a reaction. "Isn't it?"

She looked away.

"Answer me."

Min's lips trembled, but she said nothing. Her silence was an answer enough.

Zenith turned sharply on his heel and stormed from the room. His footsteps echoed down the hall, the metal beneath them vibrating with his fury. Behind him, the sterile, quiet Medbay seemed impossibly still, the only sound the faint beeping of machines and the distant hum of the engines.

And the sound of a broken girl crying tears of regret.

* * *

Quori had been pacing outside for what felt like hours, fingers raking through the data of the ASS database in a desperate search for any confirmation of their recent journey, any proof that the planets existed. When the doors to Medbay slid open, a furious Zenith emerged, and she hastened to catch up to him.

"Zenith! Wait!" she called, her voice rising over the hum of the ship's systems.

He stopped so suddenly that she nearly collided with him. His face was a storm cloud, eyes bright with anger and disbelief. "What?"

"You see," she said quickly, catching her breath, "I was searching through the database...the planets—they're strange. I couldn't find any records of them. None at all."

A wry laugh escaped him, sharp and bitter. "That's because they don't exist. We're trapped in some alternate reality created by this...thing called the Mindworm."

Chapter 16

Quori's eyes widened, shock and disbelief flickering across her features. "The Mindworm exists? I thought it was just legend! My childhood was filled with stories about it. No one outside our brethren should even know about it..."

Zenith raised an eyebrow, equally surprised. "Don't worry about how I know. What matters is that it exists." He reached into his pocket and produced the folded note from Lexicon-9, pressing it into Quori's hands. "Do you know what this means?"

Quori unfolded the paper carefully, reading aloud, the mysterious symbols rearranging themselves into legible text on the page. "'The mind is the key?'" She looked up at him, eyes wide. "What does that mean?"

"It's the answer the stupid blue goblins gave me when I asked them how to escape this reality." Zenith's tone was flat, bordering on incredulous.

"The mind..." Quori muttered, thoughtful. "If we treat this Mindworm realm as a dream, you could theoretically leave it the way you leave a dream: by realizing you are in one."

Zenith frowned, incredulous. "If that were true, then how am I still here?"

"Or..." Quori's eyes lit up with the spark of connection. "Maybe this isn't your dream. In the old stories, in order to leave a dream, the dreamer must know they are dreaming to end the dreamworld. If that's the case...we just need to find the dreamer."

Zenith's gaze darkened. "So, we're all just NPCs?"

Quori shrugged. "You could put it that way."

"I don't believe that." Zenith turned sharply and stalked toward the engine level. "Ever think about our little stowaway? Psyche. I bet she's the one who matters. The note isn't a riddle; it's a clue."

* * *

The engine room was quieter than the rest of the ship, the low hum of the engine room magnified by the absence of voices. Zenith's boots echoed against the metal floor as he approached the panel where the heating cord had been chewed through. Sitting cross-legged in front of it, completely absorbed, was Psyche. Her small form seemed to command the entire room, and her eyes sparkled with a teasing intelligence that made Zenith pause.

"Two planets," she said casually, arching an eyebrow. "And you haven't fixed this yet?"

Zenith froze, completely unprepared for her tone. "I've been busy," he muttered, trying to mask his frustration. "And besides, I lost the replacement cord."

Psyche raised an eyebrow, unimpressed. She held up the cord, dangling it in front of him. "Uh-huh. Have you tried looking behind the books on your shelf? Sometimes the answer is right in front of you."

Zenith said nothing, simply watching her.

She poked him lightly in the chest. "Denial is a river in Egypt. Keep hiding from your feelings, Zenith, and you'll drown in them."

Her words struck deeper than he expected. His jaw tightened. "How much of it is real?"

"Hm?"

"How much of my affection for Min...how much is real, and how much is created by you in this...this realm?"

Psyche laughed softly, shaking her head. "I'm not a magician. I don't create emotions. I can only warp perception. That's all I can do. Your heart...your mind...that's all yours."

The little girl read the question in Zenith's eyes before he could put it into words.

"I'm not a magician. I can't do some 'love potion' voodoo, if that's what you're asking."

"Then...what's the point of any of this?"

Suddenly, Psyche grew serious. She crossed her arms. "What do you think, Zenith? Do you think I would go to such lengths just to play games with you?"

He made no reply.

"Think about it, Zenith! Why am I making up these stupid planets and telling you these stupid stories?" She paused, gasping for breath. "I'm sure there must be a point to all of this. Tell me, Zenith! Tell me...because I don't know either."

Psyche hopped off the table and dragged herself towards the door. "I don't know! There's this voice in my head and I'm not sure I know, or don't know who it is. I'm just the messenger, Zenith...I'm sorry."

Zenith's eyes narrowed. "Then how do we leave this place?"

"The note tells you everything," Psyche replied, her tone casual but firm. "If you can read it properly, if you can think clearly...you already know how to escape. And sometimes, it's better to solve a problem together than alone. Two heads are better than one. Maybe, the answer is already in front of you."

Without waiting for a response, she pried the door open and slipped through, leaving Zenith alone with the quiet hum of the engine room and the weight of everything she had just said. He stood there for a long moment, absorbing the implication of the note and the responsibility now resting on his shoulders.

He gazed down at the slip of paper again.

The message had changed.

A final message from Psyche.

I am not the Mindworm.

The metal door slid shut behind her with a final, resonant clang.

Zenith exhaled slowly, his mind already racing, already calculating. He had his answer, and now...he had his mission.

CHAPTER 17

Many people find themselves falling into doubt. Doubt of the world, the people around them, or even themselves. Zenith had never been through such an ordeal—not truly, not in the way that strips a person down to the uncertain core of who they are—but he wasn't quite sure if what he was feeling now counted as doubt. All he knew was that there was a gnawing, clawing pressure inside him, prickling along his ribs, scraping at the back of his throat, and he couldn't get it to stop.

He couldn't name it.

He hated that he couldn't name it.

Zenith had always been able to label a feeling, dissect it, rationalize it, categorize it in a clean, tidy mental folder. Even grief had been something he could tidy away. Even anger. Even guilt.

But this?

This was new. Burrowing. Uncomfortable. A quiet, persistent dissonance, like something off-key humming beneath the surface of everything he thought he knew.

He wondered if everything he had been taught about Nirvaeliths had been false. Because Min, her of all people, shared nothing with the horrors he had imagined for so much of his life. Nothing with the monstrous, frothing creatures that populated Vaelithari children's cautionary tales. And Eros, despite everything, hadn't been like them either.

Two Nirvaeliths.

And neither fit the stories.

Maybe, Zenith thought, the stories had never been stories at all, but propaganda. Maybe he had been too young, too naïve, too trusting to question them.

The hallway lights dimmed into the ship's artificial night-cycle as Zenith entered his room, letting the sliding door hiss shut behind him. The familiar scent of oil, dust, and old paper washed over him. He stood in the semi-darkness, scanning the clutter he kept pretending he'd organize "someday."

His gaze landed on the third shelf from the top.

He shoved the replacement heating cord back in its place behind the same thick, unsightly textbook on gravitational field manipulation.

A miserable little reminder.

A symbol, now, of all the things he refused to deal with.

Zenith exhaled sharply through his nose. Fixing the cord would at least give his hands something to do, something to keep him from thinking about Min's med scan results, the tightness in her voice, the betrayal in his, the way everything had been spiraling from the moment Quori mentioned the nonexistent planets.

He took a step away from the shelf.

The door slid open.

Zenith turned.

Min stood framed in the doorway.

Her long hair was slightly mussed, probably from running her hands through it earlier. Her eyes, usually bright, observant, and painfully earnest, looked tired. Reddened around the edges. As if she'd spent the last several hours walking on careful, trembling threads of hope that he might still want to speak to her.

He wasn't ready.

Zenith's throat tightened. His first instinct was to apologize. The words rose—incomplete, hesitant, almost regretful—but he crushed them down before they could form. He hadn't sorted himself out yet. He didn't know what to feel, in what order, or whether he even deserved to feel anything.

So instead, he did the worst possible thing.

He stormed forward and shoved past her without a word. The door slammed behind him with a forceful hiss.

In the split second before it closed, he caught something flicker across her face:

A small, stunned look of hurt.

Immediate. Barely masked.

Zenith winced.

Then the door sealed, and she was gone.

He stood outside it, jaw clenched. The corridors were silent except for the faint hum of the Horizon-2's life-support systems. He could walk away. He could hide in the engine room. But his feet wouldn't move.

A sigh, light and exhausted, escaped from the other side of the door.

A few soft, shuffling steps. The creak of a mattress. A pillow being fluffed with slow, delicate motions. The thunk of someone curling into blankets.

The silence.

Zenith swallowed hard.

He leaned his forehead briefly against the cold wall.

He hated how familiar that sigh had sounded—like the ones she used to make, half-asleep in the lounge, curled up in a ridiculously oversized sweater, trying to memorize an engineering manual.

He wanted to fix this.

But he didn't know how to start.

After several long minutes, once he was sure Min had fallen asleep, Zenith eased the door open and slipped inside.

* * *

Min lay wrapped tightly in blankets, cocooned like a caterpillar, waiting to flourish into a beautiful butterfly. Only her face was visible, framed by hair that had fallen over her cheek like spilled ink. The bedside light was still dimly glowing. She had forgotten to turn it off.

Zenith approached quietly and sat on the edge of the mattress.

She was shaking.

Not much, but just enough for the blanket to tremble. Sweat dotted her forehead. Her breaths came short and uneven. And as he leaned in closer, he heard her murmur something under her breath—frantic, broken words slipping out between the cracks in her dreams.

"Test subject...no, please...perfect product...I'll do it right...don't kill me—"

Zenith felt something twist painfully in his chest.

He had known, of course, that her life before joining the crew of the Horizon-2 had been difficult, but he hadn't known that she was the result of Project Minerva until recently. But hearing it, hearing her relive it, was different.

She was the victim.

She had always been the victim.

And yet he had lashed out at her earlier because he didn't understand, because he was scared, because he hadn't known how to reconcile the false stories of Nirvaeliths in his head with the person in front of him.

Min whimpered in her sleep. Zenith's hand twitched, wanting, just for a moment, to brush her hair back, to soothe her, to tell her she was safe.

But he didn't.

Instead, guilt coiled heavily around his ribs, pulling another memory up to the forefront of his mind. One he had tried desperately not to think about.

A memory he had shoved into the deepest corner of himself.

One he had hoped would die there.

But memories never died quietly.

They waited.

And this one would wait for him until the end of time.

Or until he learned to accept it.

* * *

The smell of roasted coffee beans filled the quaint little neighborhood café on Earth. The kind of smell that settled into clothing and hair, warm and familiar. Zenith had always liked the place, not because he drank coffee, but because it was quiet. Almost quiet enough to exist outside time.

He sat at a small table near the window, picking at the corner of a napkin while he waited.

He had received a message from his friend earlier that week, asking to meet before the Horizon-2 departed.

A shadow passed across the sunlit floor tiles.

A young man stepped inside the café.

"Zenith!" he called brightly, though his tone had an unfamiliar stiffness to it. "It's been so long! How's it going?"

Zenith blinked, surprised at how different Eros looked. His friend still appeared to be in his late twenties—according to human standards—but the carefree energy that had always clung to him like a second skin seemed dimmed. Muted.

"Eros," Zenith said, rising slightly from his chair. "I almost didn't recognize you."

They laughed, shaking hands.

But Zenith couldn't shake the sensation that something was...off. He scanned Eros' face quickly: short dark hair, richer in tone than he remembered; ruby-red eyes that gleamed with an eerie, inhuman depth. None of that was new. And yet...

He was changed.

Eros sat down and took a sip of water, hands trembling just slightly.

"You've...been busy?" Zenith ventured.

Eros didn't answer the question. Instead, he leaned forward.

"Have you heard of Project Minerva?" he asked quietly, voice barely a whisper, careful to keep the conversation between the two of them.

Zenith's stomach tightened.

"Yes," he replied slowly. "Why?"

Eros sucked in a breath, like someone diving underwater.

"Because" he began, "I was the one who made the body Dr. Cale used."

The words dropped like a metal weight on the table between them.

Chapter 17

Zenith froze.

"You—what?"

Eros continued, voice strained. "I created Minerva."

Zenith felt heat rise up his neck. "Why would you do that? How could you help a man like Lysander Cale? He's—he's a monster. Everyone knows that."

Eros swallowed. "I'm sorry. I didn't want to. But he found out."

"Found out what?" Zenith demanded. "Eros, what could he possibly have on you?"

Slowly, Eros pushed aside the dark hair that fell over his forehead.

Beneath it was a hollow indentation where his crimson soul-gem should have been.

A gaping, unnatural cavity.

Zenith's breath caught.

"I'm a Nirvaelith," Eros whispered.

Zenith flinched. Not out of disgust, not truly, but out of shock so sudden it felt like someone had slammed cold water into his veins.

"That's impossible," he murmured. "You—you were always—Eros, how—?"

"I hid it," Eros said. "For years. But the doctor discovered the truth. I don't know how. Maybe he saw something in a medical scan. Maybe he recognized my energy signature. I don't know."

Zenith stared. His mind raced back through every conversation, every shared lunch, every late-night rant about engineering projects. Had he missed something? Had Eros been afraid that entire time?

"He threatened to expose me," Eros said quietly. "To the ASS. If they knew, I'd be hunted. Killed. Or worse."

Zenith's jaw tightened.

"So, you created a monster instead?"

Eros didn't flinch at the sharpness of the words, but pain and regret flickered in his eyes.

"I didn't have a choice," he murmured. "He wanted perfection. Wanted to create the 'ideal vessel.' I gave him a vessel. Nothing more."

"You made a monster," Zenith snapped.

Silence fell. Heavy. Suffocating.

Eros lowered his gaze to the tabletop. "I know. And I'm sorry."

Zenith stood abruptly, the chair legs scraping against the floor.

"Do you understand what you've done?" he demanded. "You helped a madman. You created a monster."

There was no response.

"And you've become one too."

Silence. The hum of voices in the café died away into the background. The distance between the two men stretched impossibly far. Suddenly, the scent of coffee beans became suffocating. Zenith couldn’t breathe. He strode towards the door, feeling betrayed.

"Minerva won't be a monster."

The intensity in Eros' voice halted Zenith mid-step.

"She has a pure, uncorrupted soul."

Zenith kept walking. "That doesn't justify anything."

He pushed open the doors of café, harsh sunlight bearing down on his delicate figure and blinding his eyes. He gritted his teeth and crossed the street, black tar hot beneath his feet.

He heard Eros' footsteps a few steps behind him.

"I made her for you."

The world seemed to tilt.

But Eros didn't elaborate, didn't try to explain. He just watched his friend walk away from him, sunken eyes shimmering with a sheen of forgotten tears.

The engineer looked back. Back at the friend he thought he wouldn't recognize anymore. But he was still the same Eros, just missing a piece of him...a piece that maybe, he didn't need in the first place. He met his friend's eyes one last time. Maybe one day he would be able to forgive him, but not yet.

* * *

Zenith inhaled sharply as the memory released him.

He was back in the dim room, sitting beside Min's sleeping form. His hands shook slightly as he dragged them over his face.

All these years...he had never fully understood.

Hadn't wanted to understand.

Min murmured something in her sleep and shifted slightly, her breathing evening out. The nightmare was passing.

Zenith sank down from the bed and onto the floor, leading his forehead against the mattress edge. The artificial night-cycle lights cast a pale glow over the room, soft enough to make everything feel unreal.

He exhaled, and then, finally, the tears came. Quiet. Silent. Almost ashamed of themselves. But they came.

He cried not because Min had lied.

Not because Eros had lied.

But because neither of them had ever been the monsters he had been taught to fear.

He'd always been taught that they were soulless, hateful creatures who would try to destroy everything in sight. But Eros had been different. Despite his missing soul-gem, he'd kept his consciousness, at least that was what Zenith assumed. After searching through three different Vaelithari libraries, he'd finally found a book that mentioned a similar situation. The author's best friend had been turned into a Nirvaelith, but he'd still kept his sanity because he didn't want to hurt his friend, the author.

Maybe Eros' situation was a similar one. He'd held onto his true self despite losing his soul-gem. Maybe he'd done it for Zenith. Maybe he'd done it for a different reason. But Min was likely an anomaly. She was not exactly a Nirvaelith, but nor was she Vaelithari. She was a human soul forcefully fused into a Vaelithari body, but she would always appear on medical scans as a Nirvaelith.

Zenith had wondered, when he was younger, about what would happen if he ever lost his soul-gem. Would he be able to keep his sanity or would he devolve into a soulless monster and hurt the people he cared for?

Being of a certain race doesn't make someone evil, but how they act does.

CHAPTER 18

Min woke to the sound of someone crying.

It wasn't loud—just a thin, quivering sound threading through the quiet. A breath caught on the edge of a sob. A muffled exhale that trembled like someone fighting themselves. She blinked into the dim blue of the room and turned her head very slowly toward the sound.

Zenith.

He was sitting on the floor beside the bed, his posture collapsed inward like a structure whose support beams had been knocked loose. His elbows rested on his knees; fingers tangled in his hair. Tears slipped silently down the sharp angles of his face—those sculpted, too-perfect lines that always made him look like a character carved from some storybook myth. Now those lines were softened, blurred by tears.

For a moment, Min forgot how to breathe.

She hadn't seen Zenith like this before. She had seen him frustrated, short-tempered, cold, distanced, hesitant, confused. She had seen him emotionally constipated in a thousand small ways. But this, this quiet devastation spilling out of him unguarded, was new.

And terrifying.

Her first instinct wasn't comfort. It was panic.

Not because she didn't care. But because she did. Too much.

She shut her eyes immediately, pretending she was still asleep as her heart hammered in her chest. She felt suddenly too awake, too aware, too unprepared to deal with whatever was happening inside him. And after what had happened yesterday—his anger, that door slamming centimeters from her face—she was still tiptoeing around every breath she took near him.

So, she stayed still. Motionless. A quiet observer under the cocoon of blankets.

Zenith didn't cry loudly. His sorrow came out in near-silent tremors, in breaths that caught on their way out. In the wetness dripping onto the fabric of his gloves. She heard a quiet, shaky inhalation, the soft hitch that followed. He wasn't holding himself together. Not even trying to.

Ten long minutes passed this way. His breaths eventually softened, then steadied. His shoulders lowered, the tension draining out of him in small increments, like water leaking through cracks.

And then, finally, he stilled.

His breathing evened out into a soft cadence, trying to catch his breath, regain his calm, and wipe away his tears. Slowly, the sounds of his breathing evened out into silence.

When all was quiet again, Min counted ten more breaths just to be certain. Then she dared to open her eyes.

Zenith remained motionless, head bowed, his face streaked with the evidence of emotions he never let anyone see. He looked younger like this, almost fragile. Like someone who had held up a heavy world alone for too long.

Min carefully extricated one hand from the blankets, moving slowly so the fabric wouldn't rustle. Then, with the gentle hesitation of someone unsure if touching another person was even allowed, she reached out and poked him very lightly in the shoulder blade.

No response.

She poked him again. Still nothing.

Was he asleep?

Quietly, she slipped out from under the blankets, her movements slow and practiced from years of needing to make no sound at all. The floor was cold on her bare feet as she lowered herself beside him.

Zenith shifted instinctively, the way someone shifts toward warmth in their sleep. Without opening his eyes, he leaned sideways, and his head found her lap naturally, as though he had done it a thousand times before.

Min froze.

Then slowly relaxed.

She let him settle there. One of her hands hovered awkwardly above his back before she let it descend, patting him softly. His breathing steadied even more, the tension easing from his jaw.

As she sat there, her gaze wandered aimlessly around the room, the desk, the mess of clothes, the faint glow from the data-screens. Her eyes eventually landed on the bookshelf. Something thin and teal poked out from behind a thick volume on gravitational field manipulation.

She squinted.

A replacement heating cord.

Half-hidden. Stuffed behind a book spine he probably assumed she'd never touch.

Min's lips curled upward.

So that's where it went.

Sometimes her boss had a cute side to him, albeit a catastrophically awkward one.

Her smile faded a moment later as a strange pressure coiled in her chest. A tightening. A familiar one. Her heart tripped over itself, skipping beats.

Panic.

The warning signs flared: the constriction in her breathing, the white-hot sting blooming behind her ribs, the electric static crawling under her skin.

No, not now...

But her mind was already slipping.

Dragged backward.

Pulled under.

The room dissolved into green.

A humming fluorescence swallowed the air around her. Sharp. Sterile. Too bright. Everything tinted that sickly, luminous shade that clung to her memories like mold.

She was back in the facility.

Back in the cell.

Back under that damning glow.

Her breath hitched.

She struggled against its pull, but the memory seized her anyway.

She stood on the cold platform, her wrists strapped down by metallic binds that always hummed with latent energy. The air was sharp with ozone, and the walls pulsed faintly with runes she had never been allowed to read.

The man in the white lab coat stood before her again, as vividly cruel as the day he first broke her sense of what could be real.

His face hovered above her like a pale moon hanging over a dying world—cold, clinical, and far too bright. He held a key in his hand. It looked small, harmless, polished. Its surface gleamed with that eerie medial-lab sheen.

Chapter 18

He smirked when he saw the fear flaring in her eyes.

"Observation one: fear response remains high," he said with idle satisfaction. "Good."

He inserted the key into the control panel.

Min's entire body convulsed.

Lightning erupted through her limbs. Sharp, jagged currents ripped through each nerve ending with surgical precision. Her vision splintered. Her knees buckled though the restraints held her upright. She tasted metal. Her jaw clenched so tightly she feared her own teeth might crack.

Then it stopped.

The aftershock was worse.

Her muscles twitched violently, urging her to brace for more. Her lungs refused to draw air smoothly, coming in ragged, panicked shivers.

The key clicked out of the slot.

For one second, she felt the faintest whisper of relief.

Then he laughed, the horrid sound reverberating from all the walls penning her in, and she flinched without meaning to.

"I hate you," she forced out through clenched teeth, her voice raw.

The doctor's expression didn't shift. If anything, he looked amused.

"You might hate me now," he murmured, stepping closer, "but I will be the closest thing you will ever have to a father."

Min's stomach turned cold.

"And this..." The key stabbed back into the slot.

The sharp stinging returned. Harder. Sharper.

His voice threaded through her screams like silk through wounds.

“...is the closest thing you will ever have to love."

She screamed again, throat tearing, the world swimming in that green, that awful green...

The same green of Psyche’s eyes.

No one heard her.

No one ever came.

The facility was alone in a dead sector of Old Vaelea. The kind of place chosen precisely so no sound would travel.

As she sagged forward, trembling, the doctor knelt to retrieve something that had fallen. His name tag. It glittered faintly on the floor.

Dr. Lysander Cale, Project Minerva Head Researcher

He pinned it back on.

"Remember, Min," he said in that infuriatingly gentle tone, like he thought he was a wise father teaching his child about the cruelty of the universe. "You can't trust anyone. Not the other scientists, not Eros, certainly not the public. They will all betray you."

He leaned closer, breath cold on her cheek.

"Only me. I'm your family. I only want the best for you."

His smile was too wide, too white. Wrong in a way that made her heart twist.

She would remember that smile.

Chapter 18

She would remember that room.

She would remember him.

If she ever escaped.

If she ever saw the real world at all.

The memory flickered—

And released her.

Min gasped, the room snapping back into focus around her. It never occurred to her why all her memories from the facility were tinted with a strange green, fluorescent film. It was as if she was always looking through some sort of glass panel.

The facility dissolved into Zenith's dim-blue quarters. The electric pain faded. Her muscles still trembled faintly, ghostly echoes of an old torment.

The teal wire glinted smugly from the shelf on the other side of the room.

A hand wrapped around her head, pulling her gaze down to her lap.

The same teal eyes glittered up at her.

"Don't look over there," he said, drawing a wobbly line down her cheek with his thumb. He sighed. "I can't believe I'm still scared of you finding out about it in my dreams."

Min swallowed. Dr. Cale was wrong. So painfully, obviously wrong, a small part of her was still reluctant to believe it.

There was a unique sense of safety she felt when Zenith was near. A gentleness she'd never experienced. A warmth she didn't know she was allowed to feel.

Trust.

Comfort.

Something soft bloomed in her chest like a tiny, flickering flame. Maybe, just maybe, Eros had been right to believe she could be human. Maybe she wasn't the monster the doctor had tried to craft.

And maybe, just maybe, the way she felt around Zenith, whatever that emotion was...

It might be love.

She leaned down, gently shutting his eyes with her hand, leaving just a wisp of a kiss on his forehead.

"Keep dreaming then. I'll wake up for you."

* * *

All living things have a want for acceptance, for love. We humans refer to this as a part of being "human," like the narcissistic pricks we are.

I am different. I have no need for such weak assumptions.

My creation will be no different. Project Minerva, my Minerva will be perfection itself. She won't be held back by something as futile as romance.

That is why humans are weak.

And that is why I refuse to create one.

—from Dr. Lysander Cale's notes about Project Minera

CHAPTER 19

Despite the three beacons having been planted, Zenith could only receive a decent signal from one of them.

"They could've been destroyed," Cronan said, observing yet another one of the Chief Engineer's odd beacon creations.

"If they were, I should've still received a signal. I designed them to broadcast at 21 centimeters when functional, and to emit a single X-ray burst on destruction. I'm not getting any signals whatsoever, except for the one on Lexicon-9."

Cronan let out a breath. "Well, this isn't exactly my area of expertise."

"You used M7 Relay cores, right?"

Min was standing near the doorway of the engine room, arms clasped behind her back, seemingly hiding something from view.

"I had no choice. I don't have any Lighthouse cores." Zenith held up his last three beacon cores pointedly.

In one swift motion, Min tossed a package, one that she had been hiding behind her, at Zenith. Cronan barely reacted fast enough to catch it before it hit the Chief Engineer in the face.

Zenith forgot to flinch.

Instead, his gaze remained unfixed, drifting past Cronan's arm, as if the moment had arrived a bit too late for him to remember it properly. A few seconds later, the shock caught up with him, and he stumbled backwards into a table, eyes wide and glued to the object that had almost knocked him out.

The words on the package smiled back at him.

3-Pack M7 Lighthouse Core

"I swapped the one on Lexicon-9 when I placed it." Of course, Min was always there to patch up his stupid decisions.

Cronan processed the words just as Zenith read them. "So, this is exactly what you needed. Right, Zenith?"

The Chief Engineer snatched the package out of the Captain's hands. "Get out. Both of you."

Cronan shrugged and walked out. Min moved to leave but paused in the doorway. "This time, it wasn't my fault."

Zenith knew she wasn't just talking about the beacon.

* * *

Xy'vaal had always been curious in a way that bordered on hazardous, though he insisted it was simply "healthy professional interest." As the shuttle drifted toward the dun-gold sphere of Ludus Mors, that curiously grew until it pulsed visibly through his cephalopod skin, shimmering in rippling layers. The pilot leaned forward in his seat, tentacles twitching to the rhythm of an excitement he didn't bother masking.

He wasn't the only one on edge.

Lance kept glancing between the approaching planet and the readouts hovering over his wristband, his posture subtly taut, as if he'd been waiting for something to go wrong ever since the last planet, ever since the patterns of misfortune started to feel less random and more designed.

Jace, slouched in the seat opposite him, tapped the side of his translation earpiece in agitation. "I know the name is in Latin, but I swear Liran knew this stuff better than me." His voice cracked with a frustration he'd been trying to hide since Liran's death. "It's like it's right there but my brain just won't understand."

Min, seated next to him, gently nudged the tech pad toward him. "Let the machine do it. That's what it's for."

Chapter 19

Quori, whom the team had decided should plant the beacon, peered at the glaring white screen as the antique translation software slowly whirred to life. The two outline boxes, one for input and one for output, eyed them expectantly.

"It's an old language, Jace. A couple thousand years old. You're not the broken part of the equation."

Finally, the pad chirped triumphantly.

LUDUS MORS = Game of Death.

Jace let out a soft whistle.

Xy'vaal, however, lit up like a festival lantern. "That is intriguing!"

"Not the word I'd use," Min muttered.

"It is intriguing!" Lance commented, completely disregarding the young engineer's quip.

But Xy'vaal was already halfway to imagining the dangers and delights of a planet that would name itself after death-games. In his mind, danger was just difficulty with creative lighting.

* * *

As the shuttle descended, the planet's surface came into focus: a vast, sprawling landscape of structures carved from ivory-colored stone and bioluminescent glass. Spirals wrapped around pillars. Ribbons of glowing vines traced the buildings like handwriting. The world looked theatrically ancient, like someone had taken fragments of Rome, Vegas, and a temple garden and blended them into a single marvel of architecture.

At the center of the nearest settlement shimmered a neon sign cut into classical marble: The Mystic Thorn.

"That's - subtle," Quori muttered.

The moment they stepped out of the shuttle, warm

perfumed air hit them, sweet and heavy, like the breath of some unseen jungle plant. A robed alien approached them almost immediately, its gait smooth and oddly floaty.

The creature wore a pristine white robe fastened with gold cords. A laurel crown rested atop its elongated head, which sported four glossy eyes arranged like a diamond. Eight limbs extended from beneath the robe, bending at impossible angles.

"Visitors!" it proclaimed, its voice layered, almost choral. "Welcome to Lex Vitae, capital of Ludus Mors. Come, guests. You are expected."

"Expected?" Min whispered to Lance.

He smiled back. "That's usually not good."

The alien motioned eagerly, and Xy'vaal stepped forward without hesitation, gesturing for the others to follow. And because leaving the pilot alone sounded far worse than following him, they did.

The interior of the Mystic Thorn was even more visually overwhelming, with golden inlays, floating lanterns shaped like glowing fruit, pillars carved with spiraling glyphs, and a central hall filled with long tables, covered with ornate white and gold tablecloths, where aliens with multiple limbs sat engaged in heated card battles. The room pulsed with noise: slapping cards, excited chitters, hissing laughter.

Quori slowly leaned toward Lance. "Does this feel familiar?"

"Hoo boy," he muttered. "Miraji all over again."

Before he could herd the others toward the exit, a group of robed aliens surrounded the crew, waving multiple arms in greeting.

"You must join us," said the leader. "It is the tradition of all guests. A game of Pugnare Contra Dominum."

Chapter 19

Jace's translator glitched twice before settling on: "To fight against the lord."

Quori immediately tried to turn around. "We'll pass, thanks."

Two aliens casually, but firmly, hooked limbs around her and guided her back to the table.

"There is no leaving," the leader said kindly. Too kindly.

Lance's jaw tensed. "What happens if we lose?" he asked.

The aliens all raised their many limbs, like a synchronized dance.

"We bet our limbs," the leader explained. "Tradition."

Xy'vaal perked up. " You gamble—limbs?"

"Of course!" the alien beamed. "We have many. They grow back...eventually. Does your kind not?"

"Not exactly," Min said, horrified.

Xy'vaal raised one of his many tentacles. "I have limbs! I don't think they grow back though."

"Unfortunate. But do not worry. Beginners' luck is common."

* * *

Jace rummaged in his pack and pulled out a tangle of old hardware. "Okay, okay, hold on. If we're stuck playing, we need full translation. Give me two minutes."

The antique translator whirred, sputtered, and flickered. Min knelt beside him, tweaking the machine until it was finally coaxed back to life, patching in a direct link to the crew's earpieces.

Meanwhile, Quori peeked under the table and plopped the

basketball-sized beacon into place. Luckily, Zenith had somehow managed to decrease the setup speed, allowing Quori to nonchalantly finish booting up the beacon without drawing too much attention to herself.

When Jace's translator finally came online, the alien chatter around them sharpened into meaning.

"Perfect," Jace said, exhaling. "Okay. If we understand the rules, we can win."

Quori leaned over one of the tables, examining a neighboring game. "There are cards. I can deal with cards. They look like normal poker cards."

Min looked around uneasily. The tables were packed with aliens dealing and arranging cards into their hands. She saw pairs and triples, straights, and even a couple jokers floating around. Four of the same number made a bomb. Larger numbers overpowered smaller numbers. Threes were the smallest, the ace beat the king, the two beat the ace, the black joker beat the two, and finally, the red joker was the strongest. She spotted other unique card pairings, like a move an alien called "airplane" that consisted of three sixes and three sevens. As she observed her surroundings, the pieces began to click into place in her head, and recognition slowly dawned.

She knew this game.

* * *

The rules seemed simple. The objective was to get rid of all the cards in your hand the fastest. Cards could be played in singles, or other sets within the rules. The sets were almost identical to the average poker sets, such as straights, pairs, and trios. Sometimes, players could attach extra cards to certain sets to get rid of the cards in their hands faster. The crew members would play individually, as the "lord," against three of the Ludus Mors residents.

"Who plays first?" Jace asked.

Chapter 19

"You," the leader said. "Young one with the confident eyes."

Jace stiffened at the descriptor, but he slid into the seat anyway. "Okay. Let's do this."

The game began.

The dealer began distributing the cards, each card hitting the table with a crisp snap. Jace arranged his hand like he used to whenever he played poker against his cousins, despite their complaints that he was too good at the game. His face went neutral, unreadable.

The aliens chittered among themselves.

Five minutes later, Jace leaned back, calm as ever.

"I win," he said.

"Good game," the leader replied, mildly impressed.

Jace shrugged. "I have a good poker face. And I always beat my brothers at cards anyway." He nudged Quori, who looked like she wanted to evaporate. "Your turn. It's basically some fancy version of poker with extra rules, but they're so much worse than you'd expect."

"Jace," Quori hissed, "stop underselling the fear factor here. If I lose, I'm betting a limb."

"You've got four. You'd still beat them with three."

"That's not comforting!"

Jace shoved him toward the chair anyway.

* * *

Quori sat stiffly, throat dry. Cards slapped onto the table in front of her.

She swallowed. *You can do this. You're a scientist. You can calculate probabilities. You can analyze patterns.* Just focus.

She played.

She sweated through her shirt.

She nearly fainted at the end of the round.

But she won.

Barely.

The aliens clapped politely.

Next came Lance, who didn't understand the rules or pretend to, and sat down like he was approaching the malfunctioning reactor of a nuclear cannon. Somehow, he won anyway.

"Dang," Jace whispered. "That was...chaotic."

Xy'vaal, vibrating with excitement, bounced toward the chair. "My turn!"

"Wait—" Min's voice cracked with sudden dread. Something about the last three effortless wins twisted her stomach into knots. Last round, one of the aliens had both jokers in his hand, the highest combination possible, and had chosen not to play it. "This feels wrong. They're letting us win."

Xy'vaal ignored her. "I will win! Watch!"

Min reached for him, but he was already sitting.

The game began.

Suddenly, it was as if all the aliens had gotten ten times better at the game. They all seemed to have the right cards, working with one another to bring down Xy'vaal like they could read each other's minds.

Xy'vaal lost, the round ending brutally.

Chapter 19

"Payment," the leader said.

"Put it in the bank. I will win next time."

He didn't.

Round two. Lost.

"I'll bet two of my limbs for the two I've lost," Xy'vaal said.

Round three. Lost.

"Four limbs for the four you've lost?" The leader of the aliens asked mockingly.

Round four. Lost.

He continued, stubborn, desperate, convinced he could regain what he'd lost if he just kept playing. The others shouted for him to stop, but the rules, the aliens, the room itself seemed to press against them, trapping them in their seats.

Round five. Xy'vaal no longer had any more limbs left to bet. But still, he wanted to play, believing that he would be able to win everything back.

Lost.

The aliens surged forward.

White robes, blinding, fluttering everywhere, swallowed him whole.

When they stepped back, the pilot lay shredded across the floor.

Min's legs trembled, but she forced herself to stand.

The leader turned toward her with dreadful calm.

"Your friend played an extra game," he said. A mock pout decorated his face for a split second before all his features turned serious. "And he lost. You—" All of his regrowing arms pointed at her. "You owe us one of your limbs."

"And what if she says no?" Jace choked out.

"Then you all die here."

Silence.

Min stepped forward. "Will you return my friend's body if I win?"

The leader laughed, his laurel crown shifting. "That does not seem fair, little lady."

"All or nothing," Min said. "Let the others leave now. If I lose, you can keep my entire corpse."

A murmur ran through the robed crowd. They clustered together, limbs entwining in frantic discussion.

Finally, the leader turned back.

"We agree to your terms."

He gestured toward the empty, bloody seat at the table.

CHAPTER 20

Zenith had not stopped pacing since the team of five departed for Ludus Mors. He walked the same narrow line across the bridge floor, until the metal plating itself seemed ready to snap under the weight of his nerves. The overhead lights flickered in soft pulses, synced to the ship's gentle breathing, but to Zenith's frantic mind they felt like the ticking of some unseen clock counting down.

His agitation infected the others like static jumping from surface to surface. Juno had started chewing the nails of her non-robotic hand, tearing at the skin until faint crescents of blood welled up. And Gloop, normally the least anxious creature alive, deflated into a trembling puddle of purple in the cyborg pilot's lap, making soft, pitiful burbling noises.

"Zenith," Cronan finally said from the command chair, tone carrying the worn patience of a captain who had long accepted the idiosyncrasies of his crew. "You're worrying everyone with all this pacing."

Zenith didn't respond. He continued walking, jaw tight, hands clasped behind his back hard enough for the knuckles to whiten.

Cronan tried again. "If you're worried about Min, don't be. She's smart. She's strong. She's..." he offered an encouraging shrug. "...Min. She'll be fine."

But those words carved open a memory Zenith hadn't wanted to revisit.

Project Minerva.

Dr. Cale's voice, cold and triumphant, as if declaring a universal truth, he alone had the right to shape.

"I will create the smartest and strongest being in the universe."

Zenith stopped pacing.

A shadow passed behind his eyes.

He forced a breath in and exhaled slowly, forcing agreement into his posture, into his shoulders. "You're not wrong, Captain."

But something deep inside him twisted, an instinct that always flared when Min was about to do something stupid.

He resumed pacing.

The bridge doors slid open in a sudden woosh, letting in a blast of cool air and panicked breathing. Lance stumbled in first, bracing himself against the wall. Jace followed, gasping so hard it looked painful. Quori collapsed onto the nearest console, her face pale and sweat-slick.

Zenith straightened so quickly it almost hurt. His eyes darted behind them, waiting, expecting, willing Min to appear.

She didn't.

"Where is she?" Zenith demanded, voice cracking like a whip.

Lance opened his mouth. Closed it. Looked at the other two. The three exchanged the kind of glance people share when they're deciding who has to break terrible news.

Jace swallowed hard, then stepped forward.

"Ludus Mors is...about gambling," he managed. "I-I should've known. The name, the game, everything pointed to it but I..."

Zenith's glare pinned him in place. A silent command:

Continue.

Jace's breathing faltered, but he forced the words out.

Chapter 20

"Xy'vaal is dead."

A collective intake of breath filled the bridge.

Juno shot to her feet so fast her metal chair clattered over behind her. For a heartbeat she stood frozen, then her legs buckled and she dropped to the floor, trembling, muttering incoherently as she hugged her robotic arm to her chest.

Gloop let out a thin squeaky moan, turning into a flattened blue pancake whose edges quivered with fear.

Cronan stood abruptly. "How? What happened to you out there?"

Jace was shaking. "They have—like—some old tradition, or something. A ritual game. They made us play. To bet...limbs."

"If any of us lost," Quori said quietly, stepping up beside the comms assistant, "we would have had to pay."

Zenith looked the three over. They were shaken, exhausted, haunted, but intact.

"So, I'm assuming you're the ones who won."

A deadly chill settled over the bridge.

Zenith's anger did not erupt like fire.

It froze over, cold, sharp, and slow.

But then...

It all cracked.

Psyche was watching.

She stood just behind the three escapees, half-hidden in the dim hallway beyond the bridge. Her small hands were clasped in front of her. Her pale face was unreadable. But her eyes, those unnervingly green eyes—

Zenith hated them.

He feared them.

Because they reminded him, horribly, of the dead. Eyes he swore he had seen in a photograph, staring lifelessly upward on a cold lab floor. Eyes that belonged to a girl on the news.

Eyes that felt, frighteningly, like Min's.

He tore his gaze away, forcing himself to focus.

"And Min...?" he asked.

Silence.

A silence that stretched like the moment before lightning strikes.

* * *

The aliens motioned for her to take a seat. Lance, Jace, and Quori watched from behind her, held back by the other robed aliens. The leader motioned for the others to escort the three crew members out. His laurel crown tilted gleefully as he gestured toward the open seat. Two of his lackeys took seats around the table as well.

Min pulled out the chair and sat down.

One of the aliens shuffled the deck with all eight limbs working in fluid harmony. When he finished, she extended her hand. She smiled, calm, unshaking, and terrifyingly controlled.

The alien hesitated, looked at the leader, then surrendered the deck.

Min cut the cards smoothly, split them, and began to shuffle, each movement precise as a machine. Her fingers brushed the covers of two specific cards. Her thumbnail slid along their edges, marking them so subtly that even the most experienced magician would have trouble picking up on it.

Chapter 20

The marked cards disappeared into the deck.

Three cards apart.

Lance, being escorted toward the exit at that moment, glanced back, and after zooming in on the scene with his cybernetic eye implant, both of his eyes widened.

He saw Min deal the cards.

He saw that she arranged the deck, so the marked cards went to the alien leader.

Not herself.

A deliberate disadvantage.

The perfect trap for an unsatiated ego.

The aliens at the table exchanged murmurs. The leader leaned forward, about to pluck up his cards, then suddenly pointed at Min's stack.

"I bet you dealt yourself a good hand."

Min didn't answer.

He switched the piles.

"Let's see what you can do now, little lady."

* * *

Jace, Quori, and Lance were reaching the end of the story.

Everyone waited in silence, with bated breath, equally curious and afraid of what would happen next.

Jace continued, but Zenith wasn't fully listening.

Because Psyche, standing in the bridge doorway, was mouthing the words perfectly, silently, in sync with the Jace's recap of Min's words.

Psyche's bright green eyes seemed to glow with a ghostly light.

Zenith stumbled back a step; breath caught in his throat.

The same words.

"Let's play."

Chapter 21

"And you just left her there?"

Zenith's voice didn't merely echo through the bridge, it detonated. The sound hit the walls, bounced, fractured, and kept going like shrapnel. Even the ship seemed to flinch, the overhead lights flickering as though bracing for another strike.

The Chief Engineer rarely raised his voice. He didn't need to. He usually lived in that space between silence and muttering, where his real thoughts were spoken more to himself than anyone else. But now his voice was raw, sharpened, torn open.

And beneath it was fury.

A fury so great it made room for itself where calm once lived. A fury so hot it turned his thoughts into steam, clouding them, swirling, condensing into storm banks behind his eyes. A fury made worse by the fact that none of that anger was directed at the people standing in front of him.

Anyone who didn't understand him, anyone who saw only his thin fingers clenched into fists, his strange teal eyes, and the matching gem embedded in his forehead, now pulsing with anger, would have assumed he was blaming them.

But Cronan knew better. So did Lance and Quori. Even Juno, who barely looked up from her console most days, understood.

Zenith wasn't angry at them.

He was angry at himself.

Lance inhaled slowly. "She told us to come back to the ship," he said. "And if she doesn't return in twenty minutes..." He glanced toward Jace and Quori, seeking affirmation. Both nodded grimly. "...she wants us to leave her there."

Zenith's face twisted. "She what?"

"She insisted," Lance replied. "And by the time we realized what she meant to do...we couldn't stop her. We gotta send her the shuttle. I already set it to autopilot"

Zenith pushed the three of them aside. "I'm going down there."

He made it halfway to the door before a firm hand clamped down on his shoulder.

Cronan.

The Captain's grip was unyielding. "Think with your head, Zenith," Cronan said quietly. "We can't afford to lose another engineer."

"That's not—I don't care!" Zenith spat, twisting to face him. "She's—she's down there alone with—with—"

But the words wouldn't come. His breath hitched. Something flickered in his expression—fear, guilt, recognition of the truth he didn't want to name.

And then he noticed something else.

Psyche was gone.

She had been calmly stationed outside the doors of the bridge just a couple minutes earlier, tapping her foot idly like a normal little girl.

Now there was no trace of her. Not a curl of her loose brown hair. Not a rustle of movement. Nothing.

Zenith let out a breath he hadn't realized he'd been holding.

"Fine," he said tightly. "You win, Cronan."

* * *

Chapter 21

The next twenty minutes were the longest of Zenith's very, very long life.

At first, he walked laps across the bridge. Around the navigation island. Past the planetary display. In tight circles near the communications console. His boots clicked a frantic rhythm on the metal floor.

Three minutes in, the pacing wasn't enough.

He sat down in a spare chair, crossing his right leg over his left. Barely sixty seconds later, he switched, left over right. The chair felt too soft, too warm, too wrong. His skin prickled.

He stood.

Then he was on the floor, knees pulled to his chest, the cold metal grounding him more than the chair ever could. His fingers drummed a shaky Morse code against his arm.

Around minute five, Psyche reappeared.

She didn't walk in.

Zenith didn't wait. He stood so fast Gloop startled in Quori's lap. "I know you did this. Why did you make her stay down there alone?"

Psyche tilted her head. "I thought you hated her."

The accusation hit harder than any blow.

Zenith froze. "I don't...I thought I—" His throat closed around the words.

Her eyes glinted, silvering for a moment with something not entirely human. "You're a monster, Zenith."

He flinched.

"A monster cannot love."

"I'm not a monster." His voice cracked, anger collapsing into something much more fragile.

Psyche stepped closer, the atmosphere shifting with her.

"A monster cannot die."

Then, because she was still a child, she lifted a hand, realized she was too short to reach his forehead, rose onto her tip-toes, and still couldn't quite reach the soul-gem embedded between his brows.

So she jumped.

Her fingertip struck the gem with a tiny tink.

Zenith inhaled sharply. "Don't..."

"Can you die?" Her voice was no longer teasing. It was questioning, suspicious.

He didn't answer her.

He couldn't.

He didn't speak again for the remainder of the twenty minutes.

* * *

The clock Juno had projected onto the main display dominated the bridge, its digits huge, merciless, and unblinking.

00:00:10

Ten seconds left.

Zenith wasn't the only one holding his breath anymore. Everyone had gathered around the screen. Even Kairos, who rarely emerged from the Medbay, was here, hovering anxiously beside Quori.

Gloop, sensing tension, glowed violently violet.

00:00:05

Zenith's heart hammered in his chest. He didn't need it to function, but apparently, he needed it to panic. The instinct was too old, too deeply coded, to ignore.

00:00:03

Juno whispered something under her breath. A prayer, maybe. Or a curse.

00:00:02

Gloop abandoned Quori and launched themselves at Zenith's head, clinging to his silky hair like an anxious hat.

00:00:01

A chime rang out through the bridge.

"The shuttle bay is being accessed!" Juno yelled. "She's alive!"

The room exploded into noise.

Cronan exhaled so deeply his shoulders slumped. Lance threw his arms around Jace, nearly squeezing all the air out of him. Kairos laughed with relief. Quori nearly cried.

Nobody saw Zenith's reaction.

Because he was already gone.

* * *

Zenith made it to the shuttle bay seconds before the doors finished pressurizing.

And then he saw her.

Min stepped through the airlock, staggering slightly under a heavy weight—

Xy'vaal.

Or what was left of him.

The alien pilot's body hung limp in her arms, his skin a matte, lifeless gray. His joints were sewn together with thread, cuts still wet and visible. Min was covered in his blood, blue and shimmering, like spilled starlight. It coated her arms, her shirt, her face where it had splattered in arcs. But she herself—

She was unhurt.

She was alive.

Zenith's breath caught.

She dropped Xy'vaal gently onto the floor, then wavered on her feet, exhaustion washing over her like a collapsing wave.

Zenith moved without thinking. He wanted to hug her.

The desire hit him so suddenly it felt like a malfunction. He didn't hug people. He barely stood near them. He didn't know the protocols, the choreography, or the etiquette of it. But he wanted to. He wanted to pull her into his arms and tell her she was a reckless idiot and that she was safe and that she shouldn't scare him like that again.

He almost did.

But then a whisper in the back of his mind reminded him of what had happened in Medbay. Of the words he had thrown at her in anger. Of the silence that followed. Of the way she had looked at him—hurt, confused, and trying not to show it.

His arms froze at his sides.

And then the others arrived.

Min was consumed by the group—hugged, patted, praised,

relieved over. Gloop launched themselves from Zenith's head to hers, wrapping around her joyfully. Min laughed, tired but genuine, waving away questions.

"What happened down there?"

"How did you get Xy'vaal back?"

"Min, are you hurt?"

She shook her head. "I'm fine. Really. But we need to go. Now. The longer we stay in orbit, the riskier it is."

She didn't explain why.

Only two people noticed the strange tone beneath her words.

Zenith.

And Psyche.

Blue eyes met green across the corridor, a silent understanding passing between them.

Something had happened down there.

Something Min wasn't saying.

* * *

Hours had passed.

The adrenaline from Min's return had burned itself down to embers, leaving the ship quiet in its wake. The celebration had faded. The cheering, the relief, the rush of movement...gone. The Horizon-2 drifted in the darkness like a lone lantern on the edge of a vast sea.

And Zenith was finally alone with her.

His quarters were small compared to the others'. He always insisted that he didn't need much space, but right now it felt cramped, airless, almost unbearably warm despite the hum of the ventilation system. Tools were scattered across the desk, half-finished modifications disassembled mid-thought. A coil of spare wiring lay draped over a chair, and a schematic flickered faintly on the holo-screen, forgotten.

Min sat on the edge of his bed; hands folded loosely in her lap. She hadn't cleaned Xy'vaal's blood off her boots yet. She hadn't changed out of the stained shirt. Maybe she didn't care. Maybe she couldn't bear to think about it. Maybe she was still trying to understand it herself.

Zenith stood a few paces away; eyes fixed on her as though she might disappear again if he blinked too slowly.

"What did you do?" he finally asked.

The words tumbled out, rough, unpolished, betraying the fact that he had rehearsed them a dozen times in his head before this moment and still hadn't found the right shape. His question came out harsher than he intended, but not out of anger, out of fear. Out of the echo of those ten minutes, he'd spent imagining her dead.

Min didn't look up.

Instead, she asked, "Did you fix the heating cord?"

The question hit him like an unexpected blow.

Of all things to bring up. Of all the horrors, all the blood, all the death she had carried back with her, she chose the heating cord.

Zenith's mouth opened. Closed. Then opened again. No sound came out.

He nodded.

"I was wondering when you'd finally get around to doing it," she said softly.

"Well of course I was going to get around to it..." he began, voice pitching slightly upward, defensive without meaning to be.

"You never really lost the replacement, did you?"

Silence.

His rebuttal—his excuse—whatever flimsy response he'd been constructing, died in his throat. It collapsed into dust. He could feel it, the sensation of words dissolving before they reached air. It left him feeling exposed, stripped of all the careful control he hid behind.

Min finally looked at him. Like she was seeing him clearly for the first time.

Zenith wished she wasn't.

He had lived a long, long time. Too long, sometimes. Long enough to know how to bury things, how to crush emotions into smaller boxes until they fit neatly beside the logic and practicality that ruled his life.

But this girl unsettled all of that with a single quiet question.

"Before you ask me about what I did," Min continued, standing now, "why don't you explain to me why you did what you did?"

"I—well, I thought—" The words tangled uselessly in his mouth. He could build an engine from scraps. He could reroute entire systems. He could repair a ship in the vacuum of space with nothing but duct tape and spite. But talking?

Talking was impossible.

Min slung her duffel bag over one shoulder and took a step toward the door. She paused, fingers brushing the panel, eyes drifting downward to nothing in particular.

"I don't know," he whispered.

Zenith felt that admission like a pin pressed to his circuitry.

Min paused, gazing downwards, but not at anything in particular.

"Min, I..." he tried, desperation cracking through the calm façade he usually wore. He worked through possible sentences in his head—requests, apologies, warnings, anything. But none of them fit properly. None felt like they would land the way he meant them to.

Min waited. "You didn't answer my question."

He wanted to. He couldn't. Instead, he found a question of his own to ask.

"How did you win a rigged alien card game on your first try?"

For the first time since she'd entered the room, something in Min's expression sharpened. She turned around fully, meeting his gaze head-on. Her eyes, usually warm, curious, sometimes mischievous, held something unreadable now. Something older than her years. Something that glinted almost like Psyche's had earlier, but different. Human, but not entirely.

"I rigged it my way."

Zenith's breath caught.

"And even if I didn't..." she added, reaching for the door panel.

The door slid open with a soft hiss, bright corridor light spilling into his dim room. She stepped halfway out, looking back at him just long enough for the next words to sink deep.

"I've always been good with cards."

And she was gone.

The door clicked shut.

Chapter 21

Zenith stood there long after she left, the room feeling colder than before even though he had fixed the heating cord. His hands trembled.

He didn't understand her.

He wanted to.

And that terrified him.

* * *

There is this old Chinese card game called dou dizhu I find quite fascinating.

Of all the relics from Old Earth's fractured cultures, it remains miraculously intact. Even after the alien colonization wave in the 2200s washed over the planet like a tide erasing footprints, China stayed standing. Their traditions endured. Their games endured.

Their strategy endured.

Poker is stupid. There is no elegance to it. No complexity worthy of being called a true game. Blackjack is solved by probability. Texas Hold'em is solved by patience. Hundreds of years of humans convincing themselves they're clever because they can bluff.

Ridiculous.

But dou dizhu is art. The game rewards not just memory, but foresight. Not just probability, but adaptation. To play it well is to dance on the edge of chaos while pretending to have choreographed the whole performance.

It is the perfect game.

Eros calls my fascination an obsession, but he lacks vision. My creation cannot be perfect if she is not strategically superior in every metric, including those humanity foolishly labeled "outdated" because they are too idiotic to understand them.

She must be precise. She must be intuitive. She must be capable of foreseeing the patterns in people as easily as the patterns in cards.

I cannot teach her physically—not yet. Not until the capsule is safe to unlock. But if I adjust the neurological projectors correctly, I can embed recorded matches directly into her subconscious. The subtle language of card flow. The mathematics of manipulation. The understanding of how people reveal everything when stakes rise.

She will be unbeatable.

She will be perfection incarnate.

When she is finished, of course.

When she awakens.

Oh, how I await the day I can open that capsule.

—from Dr. Lysander Cale's notes about Project Minerva

CHAPTER 22

The distance monitor, re-projected from a holo-pad, remained the same. Its cold blue digits glowed stubbornly in the dimness of the lounge, casting a faint light across Lance's face as he tapped a finger against the console. Forty-five light years. Frozen there, as if the universe itself had paused to mock them.

"It's the same," he said, not taking his eyes off the screen. His voice was steady, but there was a tightness beneath it, an exhaustion carefully folded into something that resembled composure. "Forty-five light years. Again. Still. Always."

Cronan leaned back in the chair beside the Weapons Master, exhaling through his nose in a long, drawn-out sigh. He rubbed his temples with both hands, then dropped them to his knees. "I know. Believe me, I know." A humorless chuckle slipped from him. "We need to figure out a solution to this—situation." He paused, signaling the joke before it even arrived. "It's becoming a rather endless problem."

"Now that one," Lance said. "That one's funny."

"I do what I can."

"You sure do, Cap."

But his smile, brief, barely there, softened the edge of his exhaustion. Cronan noticed but didn't comment. He was careful with moments like that with his crew; pulling at them too hard made them disappear.

Lance let his gaze drift back to the monitor. "Jokes aside," he murmured, "what are you gonna do? If we can't leave this...place? If this loop, or bubble, or whatever it is—if it's all we have left?" His voice grew quieter. "What will happen to us? To our families?"

Cronan laughed. Not because anything was funny, but because the alternative was letting the silence swallow him whole.

"What happens to us isn't important," he said. "We were disposable from the moment the Alliance stuck us on this mission. A nine-year trip through the most uncertain, uncharted region of space? It was a suicide mission." His smile sharpened, bitter at the edges. "In fact, I suspect there are people on this ship certain decision-makers wouldn't mind never seeing again..."

He drew a finger across his throat.

Lance lifted an eyebrow. "Charming."

"I'm full of talents."

"You're full of something. Maybe something and bug guts."

"Accurate."

He turned back to the console and flicked open a security overlay. Footage shimmered onto the large wall display: a quiet engine room, the gleam of coolant conduits, a stretch of dusty hallway. Two figures moved across the lower frame, Min and Zenith, walking side by side with the awkwardness of people trying very hard not to walk too close.

"I feel like I'm watching a soap opera doomed to end in tragedy," Lance muttered.

Cronan tilted his head. "You think it's that bad?"

"Dude, they're circling each other like someone is paying them by the orbit." He folded his arms. "It's literally gonna take them fifty years to get out of this...I dunno...situationship. Bro, if we don't get out of this loop, they'll never have a chance."

Cronan stared at the footage longer than he meant to.

"I know," he said quietly.

Silence settled between them, companionable and uneasy all at once. The kind of silence long-term space crews became experts at sharing.

Eventually, Lance spoke again. "Cap...if we really are stuck here, what are you going to do?"

His laugh was soft this time. Barely a breath. "What happens to me doesn't matter."

"That's not an answer."

"It's the only one I've got."

They might have stayed like that—quiet, contemplative, suspended in dim blue light—if the door hadn't slid open with a metallic hiss.

Kairos stepped inside, hands tucked into the pockets of her jacket. "You two look like someone told you the food processor broke."

"Well," Cronan said, "that would actually be worse than this."

"Objectively worse," Lance agreed.

Kairos snorted. "What are we doom-spiraling about tonight?"

Lance gestured to the screen. "Existential cosmic entrapment."

"Ooh." Kairos clasped her arms together dramatically. "My favorite bedtime story."

Cronan gave her the short version. The still-frozen distance monitor and the speculation about whether they would ever escape.

Kairos listened, her expression shifting from amusement to something gentler.

"You know," she said, voice softening, "I do hope Min and Zenith get their chance. They remind me of..." She stopped, mouth tightening at the corners.

Lance glanced at her. "Of who?"

Kairos shook her head. "No one important. Someone I lost the chance with, that's all."

Cronan's face flickered with sympathy. Subtle. Quick. Recognition flared.

Before anyone could reply, the door slid open again.

Jace entered, carrying Gloop on his left arm. The little creature bounced once, delighted by absolutely nothing in particular.

"We brought snacks," Jace announced. "Emotional support snacks."

"You brought ration bars," Kairos corrected.

Jace waved a hand. "Same thing."

Gloop wobbled in support of the comms assistant. Or was it in support of Kairos? Nobody could understand the little octopus-like creature, especially not after Xy'vaal died.

He was the only one who could.

Jace plopped down in a chair. "What are we talking about?"

"Cosmic doom," Kairos informed him.

Jace nodded. "Perfect environment for us then. We thrive on dread."

Gloop pushed the comms assistant away from them with a small tentacle. They turned green with a shiver.

More footsteps. Lighter this time.

Juno.

And beside her, Quori.

Chapter 22

Juno looked tense, the way she did when she was withholding information she really didn't want to know. "Quori has something to tell everyone," she said without preamble. "I'm heading back to the bridge. I need to keep monitoring signals."

She gave Cronan a once-over, a silent brace yourself, and left.

The room shifted. Everyone's attention swung toward Quori.

The Thalassarii scientist stood very still, her six fingers twitching with something like dread. When she spoke, her voice carried the cadence of folklore, old currents running beneath the words.

"In ancient Thalassarii legends," she began, "there is a creature said to live at the edge of the universe. A being that does not inhabit space but thought. A creature we called the Mindworm."

A murmur rippled through the room.

Quori continued. "It was said to trap unwary ships in its mental realm—an illusion so vast and convincing that entire crews could live inside it without realizing they had been caught. The Mindworm shapes the realm to reflect the fears and patterns of those within it. It feeds on the mind's attempt to escape."

Lance swallowed audibly. " That's—mental."

"It is not metal," Kairos muttered. "It's horrifying."

Quori dipped her head. "Perhaps both."

Jace raised a hand. "And you think this...time loop thing...is that mental realm?"

Quori looked at him sadly. "Yes."

"Is that what happened to Horizon-1?" Lance asked suddenly.

"Yes. I believe Horizon-1 did not simply vanish. I believe it was ensnared the same way we are." She hesitated. "Their disappearance was never a mystery of physics. It was a story of perception. They were trapped in their own consciousness."

Cronan straightened, tension tightening through his shoulders.

"And you didn't tell us sooner?" he asked.

Quori wrung her hands in a gesture of apology. "I was unsure. I searched the entire ASS archive for references to Horizon-1. I cross-checked it with Thalassarii myth tomes. Only when Zenith shared a note he received on Lexicon-9 did the final piece fall into place." Her gaze dropped. "I came forward the moment I was certain."

Silence followed.

Then...

A soft laugh.

Not Quori's. Not anyone's in the room.

A laugh from the shadows.

A figure stepped forward, dissolving out of the darkness like ink swirling into water, her green eyes glowing like embedded emeralds in the walls of the ship.

Psyche.

Her smile was small. Pleased. Almost affectionate.

"Such a smart, smart creature you are," she told Quori, voice light as drifting ash.

Her eyes gleamed, bright, merciless, and knowing.

"But it's already too late."

CHAPTER 23

Juno had always trusted the bridge monitors more than she trusted people. People lied. Intentionally, accidentally, or simply because fear bent their truths into shapes more comforting than the real ones. But monitors? Monitors just showed you what was there.

And what was there, hanging in the star-speckled void like a bruise suspended in space, was Terminus X.

At first, she thought the display was malfunctioning. That maybe the distortion of the loop for the Mindworm's mental realm was still playing tricks on their instruments. But the planet held steady, pale and veined like marble, and orb wrapped in a thin halo of icy mist. Its color was wrong—too gray, too clouded, like something drowned long ago but still floating.

Her breath caught.

"No. No, no, no—"

She slammed the intercom panel, but her hand missed. The panic hit her in a wave so sudden it shut down her coordination. Juno stumbled away from the screen and sprinted out of the bridge, her boots slamming against the corridor floor as she ran toward the gathered crew.

They were still in the lounge where Psyche had materialized. Where she had smiled at Quori as if admiring a clever student. Where she had said it was already too late.

Juno burst into the room. "Everyone, listen to me!" Her voice cracked. She barely noticed. "It's another planet. Terminus X."

Every head snapped toward her.

Except for one.

Quori turned last, because she wasn't looking at Juno. She

was looking around the shadows, eyes squinting, searching.

"Psyche," she whispered. "She's gone."

Min and Zenith, who had arrived quietly and unnoticed, stood close enough that their shoulders brushed. They looked at each other, then at Quori.

"Everyone," Cronan said, "to the bridge."

* * *

Nobody spoke on the way.

The bridge doors opened, revealing Terminus X stretched across the main viewport like a staring eye.

Gray. Still. Expectant.

Lance was the first to speak. "I bet this is the last one. It better be, or I'm never gonna get the chance to retire."

Cronan folded his arms, jaw clenched, but he didn't argue. No one needed the reminder. Every planet in the loop had demanded one life. One sacrifice, one casualty. And Terminus X appeared to be the end of the pattern.

Kairos exhaled slowly. "Well," she said, voice thin, "statistically speaking...this is where one of us dies."

"Screw it," Zenith said.

They all turned.

Zenith's expression was unreadable. Too calm, too steady, like someone who had already rehearsed this moment a hundred times inside his own head.

"We all go," he said. "Together."

Lance smirked. "Dude, that's reckless—just how I like it."

Chapter 23

"It's the only thing left." Zenith's voice sharpened. "Nothing here is real. The Mindworm shapes this place. We've been living in its illusion from the beginning. Every death is part of its game. And we don't win games by the rules."

Cronan stared at him, slow realization blooming like dawn behind his eyes.

Min stood beside Zenith, nearly shoulder to shoulder, but she said nothing. She just stared at the planet with a haunted stillness.

Kairos shook her head. "We can't rush into this. We don't know what's waiting. And if the pattern holds—"

"It won't," Zenith said.

"You don't know that."

"I do." He turned toward Jace. "'Terminus' means ending, right?"

Jace nodded.

"So, you're saying that just because the planet's named 'Ending X,' it's the end of the pattern?" Juno asked, skeptically.

"Think about it," Zenith picked up the main display screen's control tablet. He began typing. "'Noctilune' is a combination of 'night' and 'moon' in Latin, so roughly translated—"

Jace quickly tapped the name into the Latin translation software he had used on Ludus Mors. "It means 'that which belongs to the moon at night.' Roughly."

"Ah!" Lance perked up. "So...Stryx—basically vampires. Checks out."

"And you know what Ludus Mors means, I assume," Zenith finished, triumphant.

"And Miraji?" Juno was still skeptical.

Zenith shrugged. "I'd say it comes from 'mirage,' but I'm sure there's more etymology to it."

"'Mirage' comes from *'se mirer'* in French." Everyone turned to look at Min. She continued. "It means 'to gaze at one's reflection.' Miraji is a reconstruction, or in this case, a 'reflection' of old Earth. It's a representation of the inescapable truth of humanity."

The room went silent. Even the walls seemed to still, the light humming of the engines fading into the background, nearly indiscernible over the tension clouding the space.

But the young engineer wasn't finished. "Don't you find it strange that all the planets that we've encountered have names that come from extinct human languages?"

Something clicked in Zenith's brain. *Dr. Cale's daughter had liked lost human languages.* He met Min's eyes. An unspoken question permeated the air between them. *How do you know French?*

He cleared his throat, breaking the tense silence. "Moving on, since all the planets have been in theme with their names, then Terminus X should be no different."

Juno swallowed. "So, this is the end."

The bridge fell into a fragile, suspended quiet.

Finally, she closed her eyes, and exhaled. "I'm done dodging death. It's time to face it."

* * *

They touched down on Terminus X beneath a sky that looked like stone grinding against stone—gray layers of cloud stacked so heavily they felt like a weight pressing downward from the heavens. The air smelled metallic, like cold iron soaking in damp earth.

The landscape stretched flat in every direction: a wasteland of pale dust, brittle stone formations, and strange obelisks rising like broken teeth. None were uniform. Some leaned. Some spiraled. Some pulsed faintly with internal light, like dying stars trapped inside granite.

"Weird vibe," Lance muttered.

"You're underselling it," Kairos replied.

They walked together, staying close. Zenith led. Min stayed at his side. Jace kept scanning ahead and behind, his fingers never straying far from his weapon. Cronan walked quietly for once. Gloop had curled himself into a tight trembling ball on Lance's head, emitting anxious purring sounds.

Juno scouted the rear. Quori monitored atmospheric fluctuations, simultaneously trying to listen to the ground beneath her feet.

The farther they walked, the colder the air became.

At first the crew thought it was just the environment.

Then the chanting started.

Soft. Distant. A low hum threading through the air like a tremor.

Everyone froze.

"What is that?" Jace whispered.

Quori tensed. "Voices."

"Voices?" Lance said too loudly. "Where?"

But before Quori could answer, hands burst from the dust and stone. Figures in bone-white robes, faces hidden behind obsidian masks. Movements swift, silent, perfectly synchronized.

Hands grabbed onto the crew members, pulling them backward, dragging them toward a ring of pillars shaped like a circle of vertebrae. Cronan put up a fight, but a robed figure slammed into him, knocking him to the ground.

When the crew members were finally released an eternity later, they found themselves at the edge of a temple ruin. A circular stone platform rose from the ground in the center, a single marble obelisk jutting from its center, an unconscious robed figure bound to it. The other residents of Terminus X stood around him, blades carved from crystal bone held in ritualistic arcs.

"We should run," Quori said.

But they didn't run.

They watched.

Horrified.

Frozen.

As the blade descended.

A single motion.

Clean.

Final.

And then there was blood.

A pool spreading across pale stone.

A sacrifice accepted.

Min's scream cut through the air, shock and fear mixing in her gut.

"Why would they do this?" Kairos asked, her question directed to no one in particular.

The leader of the robed figures stepped forward. His obsidian mask was etched with fractures that looked eerily like cracks in a human skull.

"Everyone dies eventually," he said calmly. "We merely hasten the inevitable. The universe demands endings."

Something inside Min snapped.

Zenith reached for her instinctively, but as his hands touched her shoulders, Min's knees buckled. Her vision tunneled. The cold air thickened with shadows. And suddenly—

* * *

Dim lab lights. The sharp smell of antiseptic. Metal restraints cold against her wrists. Min stood on the edge of the examination platform, trembling with rage and terror and exhaustion. Her hands shook around the scalpel she had stolen.

"I don't want this," she whispered. "I don't want to exist like this."

She raised the blade toward her throat. A hand caught her wrist, hard and unyielding. Dr. Lysander Cale's voice flowed into her ear, smooth as anesthetic, warm as poison.

"You cannot die, Minerva."

She stared at him, voice cracking. "Why not?"

He smiled.

"Because you," he said, "are a monster."

His hand closed over hers, taking the blade from her fingers with surgical ease. Like a father removing a toy from his unruly child's rebellious clutch.

"And monsters," he whispered, "don't die."

* * *

Min's body went limp. Zenith caught her before she hit the

ground. A moment later, her eyes fluttered open.

"Zenith..." Her voice was small. Raw. "Am I a monster?"

His breath lodged in his throat.

And somewhere in the back of his skull, like a whisper dipped in venom, Psyche's voice echoed: *You're a monster, Zenith.*

He squeezed his eyes shut, shaking his head violently as if he could rattle the voice loose.

"No," he said. "No—Min, look at me. You're not a monster."

But tears streamed down his face...because he knew.

He knew what he had to do.

Psyche's other whisper slithered behind the first: *A monster cannot love. A monster cannot die.*

Zenith choked on a sob.

Min reached up, brushing a tear from his cheek.

"Then why...why do I feel like one?"

"Because someone made you believe it," Zenith whispered back. "And someone like that—someone who cages and breaks and names their cruelty 'creation'—that is the real monster."

The moment shattered.

A tremor rippled through the stone.

The residents of Terminus X stepped back, bowing their heads in unison.

The air thickened, darkening, curling inward like a tightening fist.

The tremor became a vibration, and the vibration became a rumble that crawled up boots and into bones. A large creature was breaching. From the ground beneath the sacrifice's body, from the blood seeping into the stone, from the center of the ritual circle, the Mindworm emerged.

It was no longer just a figment of thought.

It had become a creature of flesh; a story made manifest.

A towering, writing distortion, its form constantly shifting—something insectile, sometimes serpentine, sometimes a mass of eyes that saw too much and understood too deeply.

It opened its jaws, and in one massive bite, it swallowed the residents of Terminus X, blood flying, bones cracking, and muscle tearing.

CHAPTER 24

Lance had seen the soil swell before the others did. He already had his gamma-ray blaster unholstered, jaw tight, breath sharp, stance squared like he was bracing for impact. The nanotech particles of his bionic arm reorganized themselves into a miniature form of his favorite nuclear cannon model. The air around him prickled with static from the charge building in his weapons.

The Mindworm spun from the ritual site with a wet, cracking roar, soil spraying like shrapnel. Its carapace glistened with a slick, oily sheen; its horned tail snapped back and forth like a living blade. Steam hissed from the vertical seam in its skull that passed for a mouth.

Lance fired immediately.

The shots burst out bright and fast, scorching the air with streaks of red. Each bolt landed with a heavy thud against the Mindworm's armored plates, but the creature barely flinched. It just turned its enormous head, focusing on Lance with predator certainty.

Behind him, Cronan shouted for the others to fall back.

"Move! All of you—move! Back to the ship!"

His voice was nearly swallowed by the sound of churning soil and Lance's relentless firing.

Juno stood frozen, eyes wide, mouth parted, her breath stuck halfway between inhale and scream. For a second she was completely still except for the tremble in her hands. The Mindworm's scream rattled her ribs.

"Juno!" Quori's voice cracked across the chaos, sharp and urgent. "Juno, go! Get to the ship now!"

It jolted her out of her trance. She ran, feet stumbling at first, then gaining speed as she sprinted after Quori.

Jace wasn't far behind. He was already running, weaving around the jutting rocks toward the ship's ramp, dust kicking up with every step.

Cronan threw a look over his shoulder as he dragged the other toward the ship. "Lance! How are you holding up?"

Lance recharged his small-scale arm-cannon with a slow hum, but with a couple smacks from his other hand, it charged up almost immediately. The gamma-ray blaster steamed from overuse on the ground beside him. "This thing isn't going to hold up much longer!" he shouted back. "So tell your slow ass legs to hurry the hell up!"

Cronan grit his mandibles together. He grabbed Kairos by the arm and shoved her up the ramp. "Move! Lance can't stall that thing forever!"

Kairos didn't get far, not at first. She twisted at the top of the ramp, scanning for Gloop, who was still wobbling frantically in the dust like a dropped jelly.

"Gloop! Come on!" she shouted.

Gloop emitted a panicked burbling noise, which could have meant anything from *help me* to *I hate everything that's happening*. Kairos jumped, catching them mid hop, and tossed them toward the open ramp where Quori and Juno grabbed them like a slippery ball.

The ground shook again. Harder. The nanoparticles forming Lance's nuclear arm-cannon crumbled to dust. He focused the remainder of the working nanoparticles on his cybernetic eye, creating a makeshift laser beam. His final defense.

The Mindworm didn't hesitate. It lunged, its mouth cracking open into three overlapping jaws, each lined with chitinous teeth.

"Lance! Move!" Cronan yelled, sprinting toward him.

But Lance wasn't fast enough.

The Mindworm surged, its entire mass slamming forward. Its jaws closed around Lance before Cronan could reach him, swallowing him in a violent, crushing motion. There was no time for a scream. No time for anything.

Lance was gone.

Cronan stumbled to a stop. Not from shock, but from the sudden spike of pain that hit him a second later.

The Mindworm's horned tail whipped forward and drove itself straight through Cronan's abdomen. The impact forced the air out of him in a single broken grunt. Kairos screamed his name.

The creature yanked its tail free, tossing Cronan backwards. He collapsed onto the dirt, hands pressed against the catastrophic wound, blood pooling thick and fast. Jace was almost there, almost at the ramp, almost safe.

Then the Mindworm turned toward him. He skidded in the dirt as the creature reared back.

"Jace—come on!" Quori shouted, and before Jace could even process the command, Quori grabbed onto the collar of his shirt and tugged him hard, hard enough that he stumbled up the ramp and into Kairos.

The Mindworm hit the place he had been standing, just a heartbeat later. Jace screamed in shock and terror, voice cracking raw.

Kairos pulled him back, half-dragging him farther into the ship. She was panting, shaking, but she didn't stop. She grabbed Cronan's arm next and hauled his body across the ground, gritting her teeth against the weight and the blood and the way his breaths were coming in wet, gurgled shudders.

"Cronan—Cronan, stay with me!" Her voice broke. "Come on, please—stay awake!"

Behind them, the others were shouting for Zenith and Min,

who hadn't moved at all.

They were standing several meters away from the ship, staring at the Mindworm almost blankly, as if waiting for something. Or listening to something.

Somehow, impossibly, the Mindworm hadn't touched them.

Kairos dragged Cronan into a spot just inside the ship's ramp. His skin, usually so warm and golden, was fading toward greenish gray.

She tore open her medical pack, hands trembling. "I can patch this. Just hold still. I can fix this... Cronan, I can fix this—

Cronan's hand rose, slow and heavy, covering hers.

"No," he breathes out. A soft, painful smile tugging at the corner of his mouth. "You're...not a miracle worker, Kairos."

Her eyes glistened. "Don't say that. Don't—don't you dare—you're a DAMN COCKROACH, Cronan! Cockroaches don't die."

"You've done enough," Cronan murmured, voice thick with blood. "More than enough. Don't blame yourself."

Kairos' breath shattered.

"I couldn't save Wren. Now I can't save you..."

"You saved all the others." His eyes fluttered. "That's more than most get to say."

He squeezed her hand weakly one last time. "Tell my family—I went down swinging." Then the strength left his fingers.

His chest stilled.

Kairos bent over him, silent at first, just shaking. Then the sobs came, muffled and sharp, her forehead pressing against Cronan's unmoving shoulder.

Outside, the world has gone horribly quiet.

The Mindworm turned at last toward the only two left standing on the battlefield, Min and Zenith.

Min's face was pale. Her eyes were wide, but her body was frozen stiff, the remnants of her traumatic memory still permeating the air around them. Her hands shook, a shadow of the scalpel still hovering in her palms. The creature coiled its body low, focusing sharply on her.

Then it struck.

Zenith moved before his thoughts even caught up. He ran forward, pushing her out of the way of the Mindworm's strike.

Its tail slammed into him, piercing clean through his torso. There was a moment, just one, when his vision turned white. And over the roaring in his mind, a voice whispered: “A monster cannot die.”

Zenith didn’t fall. But the Mindworm tore upward, trying to split him open—

—and Zenith's expression didn't even change.

He simply took the hit.

CHAPTER 25

The others had already made it to the ship. Min could hear the remainder of the crew shouting their names, their frantic calls echoing across the blighted plain of Terminus X. The sky churned above them in shades of toxic gray, a color that shouldn't have existed, colors that didn't belong to any spectrum Min had been programmed to interpret. The ground pulsed beneath her feet as if the planet itself were a beating heart reacting to the Mindworm's arrival.

Zenith stumbled beside her, one hand pressed against the wound in his abdomen where the Mindworm's horned tail had ripped through him. His blood, shimmering with that faint, bio-luminescent sheen unique to beings made with gemstone anchors, trickled between his fingers. Even like this, dying, Zenith tried to hold himself together.

"Zenith—Zenith, stay with me," Min begged, pulling on his arm, trying to redistribute their weight so he could move faster. He wasn't cooperating. He was slowing.

He was choosing to slow.

The ground behind them was collapsing in on itself, the Mindworm thrashing deep in the crater it had carved with its hunger, but Min barely heard the roaring. Her ears were full of Zenith's ragged breathing as they ran. They were almost to the ship, almost to safety. The ramp lights glowed like a promise they could still reach, a promise that everyone else had already claimed.

And some who didn't.

Zenith stumbled once, catching himself against a jagged outcropping of rock. Min turned to steady him, but his hand came up first, bloody and shaking, and closed around her wrist.

"Min." His voice was soft. Soft in the way things became right before they broke. He looked at her with those familiar eyes.

Those eyes that she used to stubbornly call blue just to irritate him. Teal, he would always insist. A very specific teal.

He swallowed, mouth twisting in pain. "I'm sorry."

The apology didn't belong here. Not when they were still within reach of the ship. Not when she could still haul him up with her, still drag him along until help found them. Not when his blood was pouring between her fingers in a warm, horrifying stream whenever she reached for him.

And certainly not when he looked at her with eyes that seemed resigned.

"No," she said instantly, shaking her head as fiercely as her trembling allowed. "No, no, no—don't say that. Don't say anything that sounds like goodbye."

"I'm sorry," he repeated, softer this time, like he was saying it to himself.

"Come on! I can still carry you back, I—"

"I love you, Min." His teal eyes flickered like a dying lightbulb. "I want you to know that."

Her breath punched out of her lungs.

Those weren't words he said lightly. Those weren't words he ever said with anything other than certainty. They weren't a confession.

They were last words.

Deep in Zenith's mind, she saw it flicker across his face, the echo of that voice he could never escape: *A monster cannot love.*

Her breath caught. "Zenith, don't—don't say it like that. Don't talk like this is the end. We can still—Zenith, please—"

She wrapped her arms around him, clinging like she could physically anchor him to the world. Her hands spread instinctively over his wound, trying to hold the blood in, trying to keep him warm. But the blood kept slipping through her fingers, dripping thickly onto the cracked earth at their feet. Each drop struck the ground with a wet, sickening tap.

"Stop it. Stop talking like that. Zenith, you're going to be fine—Kairos can patch you up—Quori has emergency supplies—Cronan—someone—just move with me, please—"

He leaned forward, resting his forehead against hers, breath trembling. One hand rose to her cheek, cupping her face gently despite the shaking in his fingers.

His palm felt colder than he should've been.

"Min," he whispered. "You have to go. The ship won't have enough time to take off."

"No." Her grip tightened. "No—no, don't do whatever you're thinking. Zenith, please—please don't make this choice."

He closed his eyes.

That voice again, threading through his mind like a blade: *A monster cannot die.*

He exhaled, shaken but resolved.

"No—Zenith, wait—please—whatever you're thinking—don't—" Min grabbed at his wrist, trying to pull it back to her, trying to keep him anchored.

He gently, kindly moved her hands off him.

"Goodbye," he said.

Before she could react, he shoved her back—firm, deliberate, but not cruel—just enough to break her hold.

Min stumbled. "Zenith!"

He stepped away from her, standing between her and the

Mindworm.

His eyes fogged over.

"You wouldn't hurt me even if your life depended on it," he said, voice steadying into something cold. A faint cracked smile slid over his face. "So, I'll do it myself."

Her heart lurched in her chest as she realized what he meant.

Zenith reached up to his forehead with trembling fingers...

"No—Zenith—don't!" Min lunged forward.

But he was faster.

He dug his fingers beneath the glowing gemstone embedded in his skin, his core, his identity, the very thing that moored him to conscious thought, and ripped it out.

The sound was wet and sharp, of crystal being torn from flesh.

Min's scream ripped through her throat and shredded the air.

Zenith's knees buckled. The gem pulsed weakly in his palm, its light flickering like a dying star. With his other hand, he reached into his pocket and drew out a small, sharp blade. A scalpel.

He lifted it.

"No—Zenith, stop—" Min reached for him, stumbling across the shaking ground, her feet slipping in his blood.

He didn't hesitate.

The blade pierced the gemstone with a crack like breaking ice. Fractures spread instantly across its surface, light leaking through in brilliant fractures. Zenith hurled the broken gem toward the Mindworm with the last of his strength.

Chapter 25

The ground trembled. The sky wailed. The Mindworm let out a deafening roar that vibrated against the air itself.

The soul-gem struck the creature's skull and lodged there, teal light glowing brighter by the second.

Min finally reached him.

He had collapsed to his knees, eyes unfocused, breath slipping in and out like someone drowning in air.

She was kneeling before him before she realized she'd moved, grabbing his face between her hands, pulling his eyes up to look at her. His skin was cold, too cold, and beneath the iciness she felt something shifting. Changing.

His eyes flickered.

"No, no—don't fade—don't you dare fade, Zenith—look at me—look at me."

His eyes fluttered open, and for the briefest second, they were his again.

She leaned in and kissed him.

It wasn't gentle. It wasn't perfect. It wasn't anything she had ever imagined.

It was a goodbye she refused to give.

She felt him change in her arms.

His nails sharpened, darkening and lengthening, curving into wicked, obsidian claws that dragged against her back. His body shuddered violently, muscles spasming beneath her hands. His touch, which had always been careful, measured, always aware of the weight of his own strength, suddenly became violent. Primal. Desperate. Nothing like the perfect, calculated restraint she'd always known from him.

Min tried to pull away, breath ripping out of her lungs.

"Zenith, that's enough—let go—let go—!"

Her words didn't reach him. The monster inside him had sunk its talons into his consciousness.

His claws tightened, dragging her closer, his breath hot and ragged against her skin, eyes clouded with something dark and breaking. Panic surged through her as he pulled her toward him again, harder this time, fingers digging into her shoulders.

Min braced her feet, dug her heels into the ground, and shoved him with all the strength Project Minerva had given her. She was powerful, more powerful than she ever wanted or asked to be, and Zenith stumbled back, growling, his voice layered with something inhuman.

"This isn't you, Zenith," she said, voice shaking. "You're not—"

You're a monster, Zenith.

The whisper slithered across his expression. His head jerked, body twitching uncontrollably like a puppet with clipped strings.

Then he lunged at her.

"Min! Run!" Quori shouted from the ship's ramp. "He's gone! He's not himself! Min, get away from him!"

Juno echoed the warning, voice cracking. Even Kairos, still stained with Cronan's blood, was shouting for her to move.

She barely heard them.

Zenith lunged again, faster, more violently. Min dodged backward, heart splitting her chest. Her hands shook violently as she held them up between them, tears blurring her vision.

A monster cannot love.

"Zenith," she whispered, voice breaking, "I know you. You're not a monster."

Something flickered in his expression.

Something cracked open inside him.

His body shuddered violently and then his eyes cleared. Light returned to them like dawn breaking, fragile and warm. His claws dropped limply to his sides.

He mouthed her name.

Min barely had time to reach for him, to take a step toward that tiny miracle, before Quori sprinted down the ramp and grabbed her from behind, pulling her backward with both arms locked tight.

"Min! We have to go. Now!"

"No—Zenith—Zenith!" she cried, reaching toward him as Quori dragged her back toward the ship.

The broken gemstone lodged in the Mindworm began to glow. Too bright, too unstable. Its cracked core pulsing with violent, explosive energy.

Zenith lifted his head.

He saw her, teal eyes returning to their old light.

And he smiled.

A soft, heartbreakingly human smile, bittersweet and final.

One last time.

The gemstone embedded in the Mindworm's skull exploded.

Light erupted outward in a bright teal-white burst, swallowing the battlefield in a shockwave of glittering fragments. The Mindworm screeched once, as its body disintegrated into dust.

And Zenith dissolved with it, lips mouthing his final words—his final realization:

Goodbye, Psyche.

From the window of the departing ship, Min watched him crumble into particles of ash, carried away on the shockwave like scattered stars, until there was nothing left but silence.

Nothing left but the echo of a smile.

And an indecipherable message.

Still imprinted in her eyes long after the light had faded.

CHAPTER 26

The ship was too quiet.

Not peaceful. How could it be, after what they had just lived through? The hum of Horizon-2's engines vibrated through the deck plates like the slow, weak heartbeat of something barely holding itself together.

Or maybe Min was projecting. She wasn't sure anymore where her perceptions ended and the warped aftermath of the Mindworm realm began.

They had escaped.

That was what everyone kept saying, anyway.

Kairos repeated it like someone trying to convince herself. Juno said it in a whisper, as if afraid a louder voice might make the truth crack. Quori muttered it shakily while squeezing Min's shoulder with trembling fingers. Jace said it with the shocked relief of someone who had run too fast for too long. Even Gloop burbled something that sounded...congratulatory.

Min said nothing at all.

Because Psyche was watching her, pity written all over her innocent, childish features.

No longer hiding.

No longer lurking in the corner of her vision.

No longer existing like the green-tinged shadow of a memory she had always been.

She stood openly on the bridge.

Standing behind the pilot's chair, as solid and present as the metal railing she casually leaned against, emerald eyes bright with amusement. Or was it triumph? A slow grin unfurled across her face when she realized Min was looking.

Min froze.

Her stomach plunged downward, the way it had when Zenith hit the gravity switch too suddenly in the elevator, except this time she didn't land in his arms. He was no longer there to catch her. She just kept falling internally, as if her body remembered the sensation of losing everything all over again.

Psyche tilted her head.

A silent, taunting little gesture.

The rest of the crew was celebrating. Or trying to. Juno hugged Kairos. Quori wiped her face with both sleeves. Jace leaned heavily against a wall as if the ship itself might collapse if he didn't hold it upright.

"We did it," Kairos breathed. "We actually—actually got off that planet."

"Not just off the planet," Juno corrected. "Out of the Mindworm's realm entirely." She glanced up at the distance monitor in the navigation console. "We're already out of danger. The scanner shows we're heading back toward Alliance space."

"Good," Quori said, pressing a hand against her eyes. "Good. I don't think I could stand another second of that place. Let's just get home."

Home.

The word made Min's lungs feel too small.

Psyche's grin widened.

Min took a step back without meaning to. Her spine hit the cold railing behind her. The metal felt real. The rattling vibration felt real. The breath frosting faintly in the ship's recycled air felt real.

Chapter 26

But Psyche's presence was wrong.

Utterly, irreversibly wrong.

Min swallowed hard.

"Check the display," Psyche said softly.

Her voice wasn't loud.

It didn't need to be.

Min felt it slip into her mind like a knife sliding between ribs. Not painful, but inevitability disguised as suggestion.

"Min?" Quori said, noticing her distant stare. "Are you okay?"

No.

Absolutely not.

But Min forced her legs to move.

Forced her hands to stop shaking long enough to tap the navigation panel.

The screen flickered once, static crawling along its edges, before stabilizing.

DISTANCE TO BASE: 0.00 LY

Min's breath stuttered.

No. That was wrong. That was impossible. They were at least five light years away from the nearest outpost when they probably entered the Mindworm's realm. Even if the ship had jumped—had they jumped? Had something moved them? Had time warped?

Juno frowned. "What? That's...that's got to be a malfunction. It was fine just a moment ago."

Min shook her head slowly, dread washing the color from

her face. "This display is hard-wired into the long-range scanner. It doesn't glitch."

"And the base doesn't move," Jace added. "If it says we're at zero distance, then we're already at base."

"But we're not," Quori whispered.

"What about the long-range scanner?" Juno asked. "Could it be that it broke instead?"

Min shook her head. "It can't be. Zenith—" her throat constricted. "—he updated it before we left the base. It couldn't have broken already..."

"Then what's wrong?"

"Something's definitely wrong, unless..." Min's eyes darted toward Psyche. "Unless we...we never left."

Her voice cracked on the last word.

No one moved.

No one breathed.

"We didn't escape," she said, the realization pulling itself out of her throat like something alive. "We're still in the Mindworm's realm."

Psyche clapped once, delighted.

"Oh, yes, yes, yes!" she purred. "You're getting quicker at this."

Min's vision swayed.

Her knees buckled.

The world, metal and light and desperate faces, tilted sideways before dissolving, colors draining like paint running under water. Someone shouted her name.

Chapter 26

* * *

There was a girl on the ship. She had been there for as long as anyone could remember, yet nobody could seem to recall who she was. She was a scrawny little thing, with long, wavy brown hair that dragged along after her in a tangled mess, and empty, faded green eyes that seemed to be watching something. Or someone.

She never spoke. She didn't eat much either, only appearing at odd hours in the corridors, sometimes leaning against a wall as if waiting for something invisible, sometimes staring at the air above the control panels, her gaze unblinking. Her presence was so persistent, so silent, that it became a part of the ship's background, like the faint hum of the engines or the low vibration of the gravity stabilizers.

Nobody paid her any attention. Most crew members simply passed her by, pretending not to notice. Some whispered rumors. Maybe she was a ghost. Maybe she had been born aboard the ship, some accident of the universe. Some said she was the ship itself, manifest in human form. Some said she knew more than anyone would dare suspect, always present yet unnoticed, almost as if she were a pulse in the ship's own mind.

There was another girl on that ship. She was not quite as young as the first, but still innocent and naive; much unlike the first. She worked aboard the spaceship as an assistant, hired by the Chief Engineer because his old assistant had been eaten by an alien bird. This girl's name was Min.

Or at least that was what everyone called her.

"Min!"

An exasperated voice echoed through the metal halls.

"Coming!" she called back, hurriedly descending the winding stairs and clambering down the slippery metal ladders. Her boots clanged against the steel rungs as she went, the sound echoing ominously in the cavernous engine level.

From the corner of her vision, she caught the faint glimmer of someone else—a shadow, unmoving, standing at the landing above, watching. For a moment, she froze, the hairs on the back of her neck rising. The figure revealed itself to be the form of a little girl. The girl's lips parted, mouthing a silent message:

"Welcome back."

This time, Psyche did not disappear.

ABOUT THE AUTHOR

Athena Chao is a high school student from New York City with a lifelong passion for storytelling and world-building. When not writing, she can usually be found sketching new characters, reading fantasy novels, or blasting music to stimulate her imagination. Psyche is her debut novel, written between school projects, sporadic inspiration, and a lot of determination. Athena hopes this story inspires other young writers to share their own creations, no matter where they might start.

www.ingramcontent.com/pod-product-compliance
Lightning Source LLC
LaVergne TN
LVHW020714110826
845149LV00012B/2266

* 9 7 9 8 9 9 3 2 1 8 4 9 6 *